SHAMANS
SAINTS
AND
SINNERS

Printed in the United States of America

First Printing, 2015

CHK PRESS

ISBN 978-0-578-16054-2
www.chkpress.com

CHAPTER 1

A vision quest for those not ready to see

The cold war was over. Karl Richter retired from West German Intelligence, trying to put that life behind him. A decade passed. He changed continents and career, becoming a therapist. He had always wanted that.

Karl Richter was on his birth certificate. His father called him Nime, hoping the name he learned from the indigenous people in the Amazon would make Nime a child of the New World and a stranger to the tragedies of Europe. That was not to be. His involvement in the old trade continued.

It began with a request from his family. His role, because of his position, had always been to try to connect a family deeply divided ideologically and geographically between East and West, the Old World and the New. They asked if he could try to locate a long lost niece. Despite several trips to South America she remained lost. In the process he discovered he wasn't the only Intelligence Officer looking for her.

Afterward he thought that this foray into his old career might be brief. It wasn't. He was a German, and that meant to him an obligation, a moral obligation to help Israel in any way he could. Now there was Sara and Michael and a crisis that threatened all that he had done.

Michael first heard of Nime at the end of a two week episode. Michael would have called it a bender. To Nime it was more of a misguided, misunderstood pilgrimage. A vision quest for those not yet ready to see.

Sara had picked Michael up outside of Taos and was driving them in her Volvo station wagon to a plane in Albuquerque. She was 35 and slight and her jumper, scarf and short hair gave her a gamine look. Michael, slightly older, lanky and just over six feet, looked like he'd just been pulled from deep waters. He was wearing a D.H. Lawrence t-shirt, sun glasses and a baseball cap. He was struggling to minimize the wayward emotions that were playing across his face.

Sara smiled when she saw his shirt. "That Phoenix bird seems appropriate, rising once again from the ashes."

"I feel more like a Dodo bird."

"Just because you didn't find Mister Covert Action in action?"

"All I hear is Everett's retired, making himself comfortable off government contacts. A full load of bullshit, that's all I managed to scrape up."

"And that started you off."

"My consolation prize for failure."

The two fell silent. Michael finally surfaced from his hangover reverie. "I was thinking."

"In your state that's dangerous," Sara playfully cautioned.

"You think God creating the universe was the first spree?"

"Looking for some Biblical justification for your behavior?"

"Precedence, that's all," Michael said with a warm smile.

Sara wasn't swayed. "Forget it, it wasn't a spree, he rested on the seventh day, remember."

"He was already finished. It was already done. Stars, fish, people, it was done."

"It wasn't finished. His rest was part of it."

Sara caught herself getting heated as Michael fell silent. She noticed he was looking at her legs. Her short jumper had had the desired effect. He should see what he was missing. Then she had to admit to herself she was the one who had put on the brakes. Always being fair she thought and then her annoyance took hold again. "I can't believe this."

"What?"

"I come all this way trying to save you from yourself and wind up arguing theology with a man in your condition."

"Is it the theology that's bothering you, or my condition?"

"What do you think? A few hours ago you were so drunk you thought it appropriate to be having sex on D.H. Lawrence's doorstep."

"It was his Memorial," Michael corrected.

Sara rolled her eyes. "Okay, Memorial."

"As in memory of," Michael said with slurred emphasis. "Besides, my present condition is the only one where I'm able to think about such things. My attempt to be an aspiring priest seems to have drummed it out of me otherwise. It's funny because it was this very question that ended my brief career."

"The meaning of the seventh day," Sara suggested.

Michael was already back somewhere. "I just couldn't get it. I tried, really concentrated. It just set off some commotion in my head I couldn't stop. I had to quit. It's what led me to thinking that hell was God's first failed creation."

"They must have loved that bit of heresy."

"No, at the time I was inept at both heresy and orthodoxy. This came to me years later. It was the line, 'And God saw that it was good.' It finally dawned on me that he didn't know how it was going to turn out. He could have created anything he wanted. Why would he choose to make it so unpredictable?"

Sara had an answer, but was curious what Michael would say. Instead of answering right away Michael drifted off in thought. The highway's direction shifted and the two were bathed in the afternoon sunlight.

Sara pulled down her sunglasses as Michael came to, turning toward her for emphasis. "He must have known better. By experience maybe. Maybe there was a first creation where God knew everything that was going to happen ahead of time. Perfect and ordered and a huge mistake. It was like a giant machine, a real no exit kind of place. Hell was God's first failed creation. And so he created a second."

"And got it right."

"Yeah he saw that right away. So we live in two creations side by side. You can find yourself in one or the other, and despite everything I do, and I do get out there, really out there as you know, most of the time I'm stuck in the first."

"Looking for the exit," Sara added.

Michael was impressed, he was always impressed with her. No matter where he was at she could be right there. He went on. "Yeah, or the entrance to the real creation, the door that opens into life. And there are moments when it seems that a woman, a situation might do it, and I pursue it."

"Right up to Lawrence's doorstep," Sara added.

"She was a book editor and loved Lawrence. I tried to be the next best thing. It didn't hurt a bit that I'd read 'Sea and Sardinia'."

Sara shook her head in amused disbelief. "I read 'Sea and Sardinia', you just heard me talk about it."

Michael grinned in embarrassment. "Okay so I'm second to next best thing. In a more perfect world you would make love to her. Anyway we both agreed that Lawrence would appreciate the spirit of our undertaking."

"I'm sure he would. On the other hand, you must have noticed that the neighbors were not Dionysos and Bacchus."

Michael wasn't listening. He was already lost in a memory of parochial school. He was still back there struggling with it, when she asked him if he would listen to one of Nime's CDs, thinking it might do him some good. She described how they met doing work for indigenous peoples and had become friends.

"I'm not indigenous," Michael interrupted. "Maybe you're branching out into helping the indignant or the indulgent."

Sara knew he would razz her about the political correctness and her saying she trusted Nime. She was desperate enough about his condition to think that the state of mind engendered by a miserable hangover and deep depression might constitute a receptive one. Over his protest she started the CD.

Michael apparently got as far as the first lines.

"Sprees, addictions and sexual fantasy are all altered states of consciousness. They are far more than they seem on the surface. An escape, or an obsession or something that brings you pleasure. The revolutionary idea we're putting forth here is that they all have a meaning. I'd go further and say that they are an ancient and profound form of wisdom and their real intent is to transform your life."

Sara was sure his promise to listen to the rest of the CD was just an effort to get back to sleep and was surprised when it eventually turned out otherwise. The CDs were among the things found in his car which the Georgia police fished out of a river, including the body of someone he killed.

CHAPTER 2

Saving America is worth any price

There were once photographs and memorabilia covering the walls of the study of Richard Coulter's mansion in Columbia, South Carolina. The restoration of the aging house had been first his wife's venture and then both of theirs. Now restoration of the country totally occupied him.

The memorabilia he had taken down a year ago were of a family's long involvement in American military history. For Coulter, now nearing 70, what was passed on was not just tradition. There was a space where honor and courage and passions in the extreme could be expressed and tested and that his family always had a place there.

He had held them in his heart. He began to realize that it required more than the static grip of remembrance. They lived in a world made increasingly distant by the demands of his financial success. He found himself in a mercantile world, one where the days were welded together without a seam, and progressed march step with their own mundane logic until he was enclosed in them.

His disease in the beginning was fit into the same rhythm of accomplishment, success or failure. It was something to be overcome.

He gradually realized it wasn't going to be like that. It intruded into this seamless moving circle, breaking it. At first he viewed this with shock and then something deeper. He experienced a kind of despairing relief, as a barrier was broken through, in which he could sense another world and he felt their presence once again.

He removed the mementos and sat in the den with the bare walls until the voices of those in the photographs began to speak to him. They urged him to action about the country they had all served. He called Russell Everett. They had served together in Vietnam and kept in contact. Having been part of the CIA's effort in Germany during the 1980's, Everett invited Coulter to witness the fall of the Berlin Wall.

Richard, who was a fervent anti-communist from the time he read Robert Welch's "The Life of John Birch" in his youth, considered it the culmination of his life's work. Increasingly it became clear it wasn't. As Welch had revised his view over the years of whom he regarded as the enemies of the Republic, Coulter revised his.

Now Coulter had to convince others. He began meeting with like-minded people, and his house was often filled and to his dismay emptied just as often. What finally remained was a group of five.

Once again they were arguing out their positions in his study. He could have chosen a larger room, but from his experience as a CEO having the participants crowded elbow to elbow gave the ideas bouncing between them the opportunity to reach a critical mass. His illness with its attendant cough robbed his refined southern accent of its fluency, but gave it the power of urgency.

"It's ironic. All we did to defeat Communism. Godless materialists who were bent on world domination by a small clique. Unfortunately we just helped eliminate the competition for another set of jackals who are after precisely the same thing. In the process they're going to destroy the Republic and everything the founding fathers believed in. Take this trade bill of theirs. What do they call it? Intercontinental --"

"SHAFTA," the man sitting next to Coulter joked and then got serious."Five Continents Free Trade Agreement."

Richard made a mock bow to him and continued. "You've read it. Congratulations, you're probably the only citizens of this Republic to do so. It's on a fast track to destroy what little sovereignty we have left. Secret tribunals in Switzerland will have veto power over all our laws. It's the ultimate triumph of the One Worlders."

"Okay, we all agree on this. Where are we going with this?"

"We're going to take the country back".

"We're businessmen for God's sake."

"Yeah I know this isn't our stock and trade. It also wasn't the stock and trade of those gentlemen that founded this country."

The men fell silent feeling small compared to the patriots of the past. Coulter felt the energy die in the room.

"Look, I know how you feel. I feel the same. But it comes down to who's going to do it? They're filling the country up with people who give them cheap labor, don't ask questions and wouldn't know an American institution if it bit them. These people will accept whatever substitute they sell them.

"We know better, but we're getting fewer and fewer, dying out or being bought out, and if we just clip our coupons and shake our heads, we'll lose it. And the worse sin will be, we'll lose it without a fight."

"We're not getting any younger."

"Who knows? Maybe if we didn't put up with this crap, we would," Coulter joked. That brought a laugh from the group.

One of them quipped, "We'll call it Coulter's rejuvenation plan." The group shared another laugh and then it got quiet again.

Coulter broke the silence. "We don't have to face the redcoats with ball and musket, we can start with an election."

Almost as a chorus the group voiced their skepticism. "Politicians? They're all whores, bought and paid for by the same people."

"Congressman Allan Shaw isn't," Coulter forcefully replied.

"He's a union man," one of the others shot back. And then their negative responses cascaded.

"With the teamsters. Biggest pain in the ass I ever dealt with."

"Ancient history," Coulter argued.

"Okay, but he's on the left and he's on the right. Where the hell does he stand?"

Stifling a cough, Coulter quickly responded. "Out in the open, and right beside us on what really counts. You all are going to play single issue politics while the country burns."

"Well us poor Neros would like to hear how you propose to get this man elected. He doesn't have a chance of being President as a third party candidate."

"That's Everett's job," Coulter answered.

"Everett's military, he fought wars, not elections."

"You obviously haven't been involved in any elections recently."

There was laughter. Coulter let it subside and resumed. "Seriously, this is a war, on the American way of life. We can leave this country in the hands of foreigners and one worlders who have no allegiance to America, only profit. We can sit back and profit with them, but we won't live in the country our fathers and sons died to preserve."

Coulter glanced over at a photograph featuring his highly decorated son in Iraq.

"I tell you from my heart, I hear my son. I can hear his voice. Saving America is worth any price."

CHAPTER 3

Producing a fortune out of thin air

Everett had wanted to retire, finally provide for the extended family he had accumulated in his various theaters of operations. He had promised them all, his wife, the Hmong woman in Thailand, the mistress in Germany, the operative in Colombia. They had dismissed his promises with knowing smiles, but now he would prove them wrong in grand style.

Coulter had put in a call to him. He needed someone adept at destabilizing tyrannies.

There was no way to refuse Richard, he owed his life to him since that late afternoon in a field in Vietnam. Then it was to be one last operation. Coulter wanted him to help make Allan Shaw President. Everett thought it over. Among other things that required doing a Houdini, producing a fortune out of thin air.

As his plans took shape he realized a fortune for Shaw could mean a fortune for him. The more he considered it, the more certain aspects of this "last go round" dovetailed nicely with his promises and retirement.

That brought him to an airfield cleared in the midst of a jungle in South America. A customized plane sat on the runway. The head of a drug cartel, Emiliano Diaz, surrounded by paramilitary troops, waited as Everett exited the plane nearby.

Diaz could have had a functionary be there in his place. His choice of not doing so put him in unnecessary danger. It was a matter of pride. Foolish pride, he knew. But when is pride not foolish. He grew up very poor and it was the only coat he had. He still wore it.

For Everett the clearing along with its necessary evil was the site of an invisible moral line. Step over it too boldly and the ethical tension that holds you and the country together begins to dissolve. Fall too short of it and you leave the field to someone else.

Everett had gone over that line many times, his career was built on that. As long as he knew the exact coordinates of just how far, he felt he could always get back. The moral terrain was no different than a topographic one. He had turned the Sisyphean effort of endlessly climbing back up slippery slopes into a kind of moral aerobics. It tested a certain moral rigor.

Diaz was looking at Everett as he approached. Everett was medium height, had short dark hair and a military bearing that he had tried unsuccessfully to ease. He understood the problem. It was second nature to him and he had never known a first.

Diaz thought that he was like El Norte, cold, distant, clean. He and the others always seemed like they were headed for the stars. Diaz was bound to the earth and its dirt and blood. He loved it, but even he was giving his son to El Norte to go to college. He saluted Everett, gave him a warm embrace and finally a suitcase. Everett saluted back and climbed into the plane.

He checked that the suitcase was filled with hundred dollar bills and took off. He looked at the Colombians and the jungle below. He shook his head as he thought to himself. A five hundred billion dollar business. The profits going to people around the world who can only think of buying yachts and gold bathtubs. Like all problems it can be solved by getting the billions in the hands of the right people.

A call interrupted Everett's thoughts. It was a wrong number, but signaled good news nevertheless. The meeting was on in Salzburg. It was the beginning of a process that would take time, a long time, but he would remake the Middle East.

His cover story for the endeavor would be that he was brokering an arms deal for an American company. The weapon system must be significant enough for his participation to be credible, but not a monster that would have foreign Intelligence Services all over him.

Pleased he read the news feeds on his cell. A successful drone strike of an Al Qaeda leader. Everett smiled. One terrorist killed, two created. The kind of arithmetic only a defense contractor could love.

The inevitable Blowback. The Saudis will buy drones for their fanatical friends. The new and improved Al Qaeda Air

Force. It'll just be a matter of time, these mechanical birds will come home to roost. That is unless he was successful and this threat would cease to exist.

Thinking about the drones helped him fill in some of the details of his plan for Salzburg. He'd equip himself with tech specs and a glowing brochure of a cutting edge drone from a defense technology conglomerate.

The full color pictures would contain a digitally encoded message. The secret document embedded within them, a mere collection of words and signatures, would be far more dangerous than any weapons system.

CHAPTER 4

Cast away memory and consequence and you're
so light you can fly

The DEA had been an ideal choice for Michael. It was a clear cut moral universe where he could exercise his drive to succeed and his tireless pursuit of drug dealers. Maintaining that burning intensity helped clear the plague of intrusive thoughts that filled his head.

His ceaseless, single-minded focus didn't go unrecognized. He was the type of gungho agent they nicknamed Y.A.'s. Officially it stood for Young Ahabs, unofficially for Young Assholes.

Most of the other agents outgrew it. They got married, had kids and changed. He got married, had a kid and didn't. He made the agents uncomfortable and they regarded him as a danger.

He ignored them. He knew the real danger was nebulousness. Life had to have a point, like fire needed oxygen to keep burning. Without it there was emptiness. It didn't matter if it was the kind that ached or just made the days drift.

In 2000 he was part of Clinton's Plan Colombia constructing a career making case, tying drug dealers to a right wing paramilitary chief. To his satisfaction it was going well. Too well as it turned out. His supervisor called him into his office and warned him off the case. It was a matter of national security he was told.

He angrily responded that the security of the most powerful nation on earth didn't require protecting drug dealers. The two other agents assigned to the case agreed with Michael, but refused to join him in going ahead with it.

He chose the surprise of early morning to go in. The dealers were tipped off and told to clear out. Instead they stuck around and ambushed him for fun. He was shot in the leg.

Disabled, he was offered a desk job for better pay. He was strictly a street agent. He knew the bogus job was offered for his silence. His only interest in taking it was the chance to follow up on his own case. He pursued it relentlessly to the exclusion of everything else and wasn't silent. Michael was let off with a disability.

The pursuit was over. The chase was over. Crippled and bitter that he was set up, he was driven to find out who did it. The passion soon became an obsession. Although his reconstruction of what had happened made progress, leading him from a drug cartel to an intelligence operative named Everett, his haranguing made enemies even of his friends and finally of his wife as they got their divorce.

He would prove them all wrong. He would get his man. Nothing would deter him, not his drinking, not his lack of sleep, after all the Pinkertons never slept. He was desperate for any lead and chased down the few he got. And when they turned out to be shadows, the chase would turn into a spree.

What he was doing and what he thought he was doing parted company. Good riddance. All confusion and agony burnt up in an all consuming passion.

It led to situations sometimes romantic, sometimes brutal. Waking up not only wondering where he'd been, but who he'd been. Living with recollections vague and not so vague. Like the one of a naked young woman over the back of his car in the middle of nowhere swearing at him somehow laughingly, angrily and lewdly at the same time. And women who wanted poetry underneath the moon and women who thought a black eye was sexy underneath their sunglasses.

It always started the same way as the sight of some woman suddenly pierced him, filling him with an impossible longing, a feeling so intensely painful it seemed like a knife wound.

The piercing visions multiplied, leading him on a spree from one woman to the next as he started to drink heavily and take uppers. Some of the women realized he wasn't there, some were as adrift as he was.

It was like defying gravity he described later, cast away memory and consequence and you're so light you can fly. But for how long? It doesn't matter, gravity is in league with the ground and we'll all end there soon enough.

When Michael eventually came to he was mortified to see the shape he was in. Getting some rest would have helped, but when he slowed down his body felt like an ill-fitting suit.

He occupied his sleepless nights with radio. He would sit in the dark listening to a montage of voices and music. It helped fill the silence, but didn't touch him.

His nightly montage of listening finally led to his hearing Sara's program. He was amused by her opening lines. "This is Inside America, where you the listener help uncover the truth."

"The blind leading the dame" he would joke every time he heard her intro.

He became something of a regular listener to her twice a week broadcasts. Not because of the show's content which he dismissed thoroughly. He was held by a quality in her voice. It was painful hearing how naive and earnest she was. He tuned in every so often he told himself to see if she got any better background information, but more likely hoping to see she had lost some of her earnestness.

That she didn't needled him. It challenged him in a way he didn't like. He would have stopped listening had he not heard her mention Everett.

He must have been only half listening because it seemed to come out of nowhere, said in passing in a list of people long familiar to him. It riveted him, hearing a name that seemed to exist only inside his head. He was impressed that Sara was able to piece together as much of his history as she did.

His private drama had gone public. He wasn't alone, somebody else was in the chase. And then he realized that she was in the chase and he wasn't. It hit hard. He decided to do something about it.

CHAPTER 5

Congratulations, you managed to get shipwrecked
in the middle of a desert

Michael began with the limited intention to check out the information Sara had uncovered. It wasn't much of a start but it reignited his commitment to get Everett. He reestablished contacts he had in his years at the DEA. A good deal of his work was in using bank officials, informants, and hackers to trace money laundering, follow the money trails.

All of them were surprised and not exactly happy to see him again. He no longer had the institutional clout of the DEA. He relied on a few old debts owed him, but mainly on the persuasiveness of remaining silent about their present activities.

He created an intricately detailed hierarchy out of the photographs and data, and he watched it, the comings and goings of dummy corporations, offshore holding companies, Swiss bank accounts and wiretaps.

He had an admiration for the historians and researchers he read. It was an art to reconstruct history out of a swamp of information. But he wasn't interested in adding to speculative history. He wanted to catch Everett in the act. He wanted to draw blood.

The cost of his research ate up his disability checks. Out of necessity he started a private security business. His interest in it was nil, but he did rather well anyway. It was just as an acquaintance had told him. "This one even you can't screw up. You got fear as your silent partner."

He called Sara after a program she did on the DEA and talked to her for an hour an a half. It was journalist's dream. They met for coffee.

Sara had successfully occupied an underinhabited niche as a liberal voice in radio. She was outgoing, bright, and ivy league educated. She had met her husband Jack in law school as she was preparing to be an activist lawyer. It turned out she was bored with practicing law.

Jack thought with her engaging personality she should try the media. He had friends who owned a radio station. His initial idea was a radio show with her answering questions using her law background. It was obvious her real interests were political so the idea soon became "Inside America", a talk show with a liberal slant. The politics didn't match the owner's views, but Jack convinced them it was good business.

It wasn't. Engaging in person, Sara was stiff and shy on the air. The show was kept on as a personal favor. Her improvement was slow. It didn't help that her marriage was breaking up. At her worst she thought Jack had devised the radio show to make himself feel less guilty about having his affairs. "I've got to hand it to you. You're the only person who could be having an affair and still be controlling."

Not long after they separated Michael called the show. His wealth of background information helped her confidence. He made her nervous with his intensity, but she sensed a chemistry between them and asked him to be a guest on the show. He was knowledgeable, controversial and funny. The show clicked which led to his being a regular, almost a co-host.

They started having an affair. Michael's raw edges made for good sex, but he was too turbulent for someone trying to sort out her new life. She sensed he wasn't all there, but certain moments hinted at something inside. Nothing he wanted to deal with.

"Don't you ever think about things?" she asked him.

"They already bug me enough, they don't need my help."

The two let the affair pass by, but they remained friends.

It was a friendship that was tested. Michael used up his backlog of information and wasn't getting anything new. When he got frustrated and desperate, he took his customary way out. Sara picked him up in cities from Cambridge to Durham and helped him recover from the episodes.

It didn't seem to effect his performance on the show. If he was less informative he was more witty. It still worked except for Michael. Sara tried to reassure him as they crossed the parking lot to their cars after a ragged show. Michael wasn't reassured. "The show wasn't bad, I was."

"You were okay," Sara responded. "I loved your line. His idea of gun control is have a steady aim. We just couldn't get beyond the flak to the real issues. We couldn't raise a whisper about the trade bill. Nobody seemed to get it, even after your NAFTA on steroids."

The two were interrupted by the honk of a convertible passing in the street. They turned and saw a young man and a woman waving an enthusiastic greeting to them. They looked like an All American couple out of Norman Rockwell. Sara waved back.

"Fans of yours?" Michael asked as the couple drove off.

Sara shrugged. "I have them everywhere. Five in California, three in Indiana, four in Delaware."

"Very funny," Michael responded. "But after my fabulous performance tonight, I think it's going to be two in Delaware. Your listeners were more with it than I was. I thoroughly muffed the election question."

"It's a long way off, and what can you say? We've got tweedledum and a field of tweedledees stretching from New Hampshire to California."

"Not if Allan Shaw is in the picture. They asked me a very simple question, do I think he's going to run? Simple if you know where the money's coming from."

"So you gave an educated guess," Sara offered.

Michael frowned. "I wouldn't have to guess if I knew."

"You're working on it."

"It's a good line, I use it often. I'm not getting anything from the usual sources. Either they've gotten damn good at keeping quiet or I'm going deaf. I've got to take some time off, see if I can come up with something."

Sara knew what that meant, but she didn't say anything. In a week he did actually produce a lead. A small one. He got a tip that a financial adviser to Everett was part of a group of investors interested in a beer company. It wasn't much, but you never know.

Through his contacts he checked what it looked like on paper. Everything was upfront. No offshore assets. No dummy corporations. There were no promising signs anywhere. There was nothing here and he knew it.

He drove out to the brewery to confirm the obvious. A tour was going on and a group of people were being lectured in front of the huge stainless steel fermentation tanks. Michael paused to listen for a few minutes and then went to talk to the brew master.

He was open and excited about the new owners. Everett was thinking about retiring. Some friends of his were trying to set him up with good investments, like a string of craft breweries that could be made enticing to a conglomerate.

The brew master offered Michael some samples of his art. He remembered Everett and liked him and his enthusiasm. The others were interested only in finances. He was an amateur beer maker and wanted to talk about the process.

Michael left. He decided to do some more sampling at a local bar. It didn't improve his outlook. He was depressed. Not only that checking this out had been pretty desperate, it was hearing the words retire and Everett together.

He ordered another beer and considered his ultimate nightmare, Everett retiring. The thought of him just getting up and walking away from all this. Where would all that leave Michael? Even if he killed him it would be like killing some-body already dead. It gave him the shudders thinking about people changing like that. Permanent.

He was being ridiculous. What's the big deal about change? Sure he changes every time he takes a drink, but you have a few drinks, change scenery a bit and next morning you're back the same. Or are you? He didn't linger long on that thought.

There was a woman sitting at a table nearby, reading a book. "So who am I competing with?" Michael said by way of introduction.

* * *

Two days later Sara was driving to Taos to pick him up. Her Volvo had a definite lived in look. There were toys, radio show manuscripts and a wrapped painting on the back seat. She was thinking about her life as she admired the red mesas set off against a brilliant blue April sky. The mesas were once under water. Life's definitely about change. Just wish my life had a little less.

At least Michael is picking nicer spots to fall to earth. Maybe Nime's CDs will help. Jack, it's still hard. Easier if I didn't see him, but he's great with the kids. They need it. Still hoping we'll get back together.

Parents broke up. Why I'm good at picking up pieces. Years of practice. I make a mess and then I pick up the pieces.

I thought if you knew the past you weren't condemned to relive it. Must be a different kind of knowing. There's knowing in your head that fire burns and there's the kind of knowing when you put your finger on a hot stove and your hand pulls away. Must be more like that. Knowing it in your bones. How do you do that? Might have to settle for reminder notes on the refrigerator.

What happened to something working for a change? What about the show, the children? Can't take credit there. Seem to work in spite of how I screw up. There you go.

She repeated two lines her friend Ann had given her that helped. "Today has never been done. Go easy on yourself."

Sara had wired the bail money. Michael was waiting in the shade in front of the City Hall as she pulled up. It was an unseasonably warm day and there was no soft breeze to shift the sun's focus. He seemed to stagger under its glare as he walked unsteadily over to Sara's station wagon.

"Congratulations, you managed to get shipwrecked in the middle of a desert," Sara joked as they drove off.

"We were just trying to follow a mighty river to its source. What can I say?"

She smiled as she took in his appearance. Michael noticed her smile. "She loved Lawrence and I wanted to be Lawrence for her." He tugged at his t-shirt. "Probably the most innocent form of fetishism I've ever practiced."

"How gallant," Sara said trying to keep her jealousy in check by remembering she chose to cool off the relationship. "I remember you had a thing for my high heels." His expression told her she could have used the present tense. There was a fraught silence between them.

Michael self consciously adjusted his cap. "It's all part of my feeble mystical attempt at having a thing for everything."

"And who did you want her to be?" Sara asked, enjoying, despite herself, treading on dangerous ground.

"I don't know. She was southern, maybe she could have been Anabelle Lee. She was doing just fine as herself."

"Where'd you meet?"

"My mouth and her mouth, my mouth and her thighs, her mouth and..."

"Location, location, location," Sara intoned with an edge.

"In a bar. I was sitting there thinking about this lead, but it looks for all the world like they took over a beer business, plain and simple. I kept going over it, but I was empty and dry as that field over there. Then it begins like a few drops of rain and right away it turns into a flood. Every woman from there to here's going on in my head with every idea you could think of."

"Including Miss Lee," Sara said, sharper than she wanted.

"We made quite a fire, but I think she was disappointed it was only Michael Flaherty who emerged from the ashes."

"Were you expecting anything different?" Sara challenged.

"I always seem to," Michael responded too easily.

The two drove on, Michael unsettled by his response. As they neared Albuquerque Sara played the CD for him.

"Sprees, addictions and sexual fantasy are all altered states of consciousness. They are far more than they seem on the surface. An escape, or an obsession or something that brings you pleasure. The revolutionary idea we're putting forth here is that they all have a meaning. I'd go further and say that they are an ancient and profound form of wisdom and their real intent is to transform your life."

Michael thought for a moment and then turned off the sound. "Is he for real?"

Sara batted the question right back. "Used to be high up in West German Intelligence, is that real enough?" Even half there Michael was now fully interested.

Sara saw him waiting for an explanation. "We were both working on a Huichol Indian project. He found out I had a radio show and listened and like you felt sorry for me. He helped me out and every so often I run something by him."

"We're you involved?"

"He's married. Not like my marriage, your marriage. But married married."

Michael considered this for a moment and then clearly elsewhere turned the sound back on.

"It's an obsession because we don't get the message. So it keeps repeating itself over and over like a person trying to make themselves heard by someone hearing impaired."

Michael seemed to reach a conclusion. He was suddenly very serious as he shut off the CD. "I know I'm right about Everett. If I was half as good at penetrating the secret of my own life I'd be on cloud nine or ten. I'm going to use your radio show to flush him out."

Sara made a face. "Just remember there are libel laws in this country."

"What I remember is that he destroyed my life and I'm going to return the favor."

CHAPTER 6

*It's not the sort of thing that goes bang and lights
up New Mexico. But it could change the world if
it was ever used.*

Everett would never have called it the University of California. It was always Berkeley. He didn't think of it as a school, but simply as one of the capitals of the opposition and had never been there. That he was going there now amused him.

He had an appointment to see a research botanist named Rehema Boulat. He had heard of her years ago, but only as a member of a left wing political group. As he went through Sather Gate and crossed the campus he thoroughly enjoyed the irony that he was going to a place where he he had been particularly reviled, to see a black woman radical who had hated him and all he stood for. That's what he liked about life, nothing too absurd it wouldn't throw it at you.

Her office door was open and she was searching her ipad as she spoke on her cell. She motioned for him to enter. He closed the door behind him and locked it. On the wall were a series of 19th century botanical illustrations and a poster of Malcolm X.

Finding what the caller was asking for, Rehema got off the phone. Everett was looking at the poster. Rehema didn't bother with a phony greeting. "You assassinated him. Not you of course."

"Do you expect me to apologize?"

"I expect you to have some tidy explanation."

"Tidy costs no extra, so here it is," Everett joked. Rehema grimaced and he went on. "Malcolm would have appreciated my position. By any means necessary. And that should be your position, even if it happens to be me. These drugs are killing your people."

"You ought to know all about that. Our man in Ilaponga. Was it just advisory or did you actually help them load the cocaine?"

"They're enterprising sort. They would have sold it with or without our help. This way our scum beat their scum, and you and I can have this pleasant chat in peace and freedom."

"I'm sure you always have a handy rationale."

"Never leave home without one."

Rehema let Everett's flippancy go by. "Why pick on me? I'm hardly the only one doing this research." Rehema found a database on her ipad and started to hand it to Everett.

Everett didn't take it. "All of your associates are busy hiding their consciences behind 'Top Secret'. They got paid for their research and their silence keeps them getting paid. They're a bright bunch, but they're not going to get any prize for bucking the system."

"Why should I trust you?"

"Because Allan Shaw is going to run for President and he trusted me to help him win the war on drugs."

Everett's sudden openness hit Boulat like a blow. She was sure Everett's connection with Shaw was a secret, a dangerous one at that. She thought over Everett's revelation. "Why did you tell me that?" she said with a good deal of suspicion.

Everett tried to allay it. "I want you to go to the wall for this, and I wanted to show you I'm willing to do the same."

Rehema handed Everett a file of research papers. He began looking them over. "Black Forest, that's perfect, your name?" She nodded.

"How long have you been working on this?"

"Since I was six."

"You and Mozart."

"Not quite, I didn't write any symphonies. I just noticed the chestnut tree in our front yard was dying and wondered why."

Everett sat down in a chair by the window and continued reading. "This all got started with good old chestnut blight?"

"It's no joke. Around 1900 a fungus came into the country on a shipment of botanical specimens from Japan. It started infecting the chestnut trees and spread like wildfire. It killed millions of trees, including the one that was dying in our front yard."

"Pretty good for a six year old."

"No, that just got me interested in botany. I didn't make this connection until much later. It wasn't until I'd been involved in studies about the lack of biodiversity."

"You mean the rain forest thing?" Everett offered.

"No, that's a real problem, but this is a different one. The whole world's food supply depends on massive plantings of a very few strains of wheat, corn, and rice. Something could come along like a chestnut blight to wipe out everything we grew in the ground. It would mean using sterilized cell culture to grow our food in factories. Not very economical unless you can pay a hundred dollars a pound for corn."

Everett glanced up from his reading. "You're hitting close to home. I can skip corn flakes, but I hate to see Jack Daniels go through the roof."

Rehema couldn't hide her anger. "I thought your interests were only in harder drugs."

"The millions of acres of that," Everett said pointing to the illustration of a coca tree on her wall.

"No wonder you recognized it, I'm sure you've had plenty opportunity to-."

"Let's deal with this opportunity," Everett interrupted.

Rehema checked her anger and went on. "One day it crossed my mind, what about the plants we're not so crazy about? If there's something in nature that will kill a tree you love, why not one that will kill a tree you're not so crazy about?

"Genetic engineering means it can be extremely lethal and we can target any plant we want and only that plant."

"So it's a possibility. Is it more than that?"

"It doesn't involve any great breakthrough scientifically, much more of a political problem than a scientific one. It's not exactly the sort of thing that goes bang and lights up New Mexico. But it could change the world, if it was ever used."

"It'll get used." Everett's sotto voce response was adamant and reflected the certainty of a man used to making things happen. He went on. "Either we'll do it or you will have forced the government to do it. Either way you win. It means a new life for your people. No drug gangs ruling your neighborhoods, no lives ruined, no children killed on their doorstep."

Rehema thought it over as Everett got up and put the papers on her desk. "In the meantime we'll keep an eye on you. It'll be a dangerous time until it's announced."

"I remember speaking to a colleague at the University of Arkansas about going public with it to get some action. He said he didn't want to come out every morning and look under his car for a bomb."

"Any second thoughts?"

"Is that a serious question?"

"Not really, considering what I know of you. But I had to ask anyway."

* * *

The secrecy of Everett's meeting was compromised in less than twenty four hours. Emiliano Diaz heard the news on his way to a mountain resort outside of Bogota. The news of course didn't come to him first. He was now retired. The Colombian government needed to show some results in its war on drugs and he was the oldest of the cartel leaders and his power was waning. He chose retirement rather than arrest.

Diaz wondered what the men who replaced him would do with the news. Something stupid. The news came from very reliable sources in the American Mafia, but it came easily. He didn't trust easy.

CHAPTER 7

It's a shame you have to die in a drama beyond
your understanding, but then don't we all.

The cabin was in a part of Idaho that was once remote. The neighbors said it was built in the 1930's completely out of stone by someone inspired by Robinson Jeffers. The isolation suited him as well as the privation of the depression. Twenty years later prosperity ended that dream as the development of the fifties drove him away to nobody knows where.

Steve Langford had rented it for the summer. The locals liked him. He had funny stories about the life in the East Coast he was escaping, wasn't too handsome, too bright or too much anything and he listened.

The bedroom was romantically lit by moonlight as he and Patty Briggs were in bed. Patty was nineteen. She worked at a local bar and was model pretty enough to enjoy being mistaken for an actress. She had told a girlfriend he was a breath of fresh air and they both laughed considering this was supposed to be fresh air country. Steve was twenty six.

"You're sure something," he complimented her.

"That's what I expect to hear from the guys up here. I thought you were different." She was irritated that he had to rush her off in an hour to go to another meeting. He didn't even seem the type.

"Sorry."

They began making love. Suddenly she froze as she saw a thin beam of laser light trace its way along her body.

"Who's there?"

"A jealous patriot," a voice responded from the darkness.

Shocked, the two anxiously looked up and saw Martin Arens seated in a chair, partially concealed in shadow. Arens was in his early forties, sandy haired and had an almost languid grace. His appearance was parceled out as if life and death had had equal claims on him. His body, despite years of physical training, was soft and sensual. His features were hard, chiseled to the point that the artist might have been doing a death's head, except for his vibrant blue eyes that seemed to laugh at the death surrounding them.

He aimed his gun's laser sight at Patty's forehead. Patty was terrified. Steve was busy weighing their options as Patty spoke. "You're not in the militia, what do you want?! There's money in my purse."

"I'm not in the militia, but neither is lover boy," Arens replied. "He's with the FBI."

Patty was frightened and bewildered. "What's he talking about?" Steve was silent, focusing on his jacket hanging on a chair nearby.

"Please don't hurt me," Patty pleaded.

Aren's response was cold but tinged with sympathy. "It's a shame you have to die in a drama beyond your understanding, but then don't we all."

In a single motion, Steve threw a pillow at Arens and lunged toward his jacket and a gun. Arens deflected the pillow. He watched Steve's movement as if captured in a series of stills. He waited for the still in which Steve had his gun in hand before killing him with one shot. He was chiding himself about his slightly faulty aim as he shot Patty.

Having killed the pair, Arens entered the kitchen and surveyed it. He returned to the bedroom and dipped his fingers with the blood from Patty's head wound. Going back in the kitchen, he began painting the refrigerator door with his bloodied fingers.

He stepped back to judge his handiwork. It was a militia symbol, a rattlesnake and the words, "Don't Tread on Me". He smiled appreciatively at what he saw. "I don't know much about art, but I know what I like."

As Arens walked away from the cabin he began singing a ditty to the tune of "Over There".

"Heidegger, Heidegger,

For the angst is coming, the angst is coming,

And they'll soon be fear and trembling over there.

So beware, no exit there,

For the angst is coming, the angst is coming,

And they'll soon be fear and trembling over there."

CHAPTER 8

The only war our government is winning is the
war on the American people.

A photograph of Arens was on the wall of a loft in down-town Philadelphia. He was one face among thousands as part of a wall consuming collage of photos of organized crime, the intelligence community, militia and fringe groups. In an attempt to order this Byzantine universe the collage was criss-crossed by a web of hand drawn lines and scribbled notes.

A worktable littered with electronic surveillance equipment, computers and cameras ran nearly the length of the wall adjacent. Jazz music was coming from a set of speakers.

Michael was on an exercise machine, strengthening his bullet scarred right leg. He was in a pair of shorts and shirtless and he was in pain. His landline rang and a voice came from the answering machine. "Flaherty, this is Mr. Donaldson. That fancy alarm is so sensitive it goes off whenever the damn dog barks. I don't know whether to shoot you or the dog."

Michael ignored the message. He got off the exercise machine and talked to his leg. "What's it going to be, good day or bad?" Michael tested his leg and winced. He began to massage it as he checked his cell for texts. He was pleased at what he read.

He dressed quickly. He had an important lead to tell Sara and was definitely going to be early for this show. Leaving the loft, he scooped up his mail.

A letter addressed to his son had come back "return to sender". He knew it would like the others he'd sent. The pain he felt over his repeated attempts was a form of penance. What he'd do if he actually had to communicate, he had no idea.

As he maneuvered his vintage Camaro through gridlock, he glanced down at the set of CDs Sara left with him. He'd been avoiding it. That had worked until now. It was becoming too obvious to him that he was avoiding it and that got his pride. Dismissing it without listening wouldn't do. He'd have to listen at least once and shoot it down point by point as he had some of her other finds. He started the CD.

"I know it's hard to believe the cast of characters you find in fantasy have anything to tell you, but they do. Believe it or not I think that 's why they're here. They are intermediaries between you and the sources of your life.

"The mysterious stranger occurs often in fantasy. It's a perfect symbol of that part of ourselves that is hidden, disowned, forgotten. We are indeed estranged from our powers, our possibilities. So this mysterious stranger has a lot to tell us, to give us.

"We begin with a tension, a longing. The tension we feel is the gap between where we are and the possibilities of our becoming. Sexual release is a momentary arc across that gap. It's temporary because it occurs too rapidly to permit any awareness to be brought to it. Like visiting 10 European capitals in three days. A blur.

"It comes and it goes and we are moved by it, but we can't see into the heart of it. And that's what understanding our sexual fantasies allows us to do. It allows us to make a journey in that gap with awareness and connect to the deepest sources of our life."

Michael shut off the CD. He drove the rest of the way to the station sorting out his reaction. If he hadn't been stuck in a car he would have been pacing, stopping only for a sip of coffee. It reminded him of something. It was that funny feeling he got trying to break a case and what he needed was right in front of him and he walked right past it.

This was worse. It was not just right in front of him, it was screaming at him, driving him crazy to get his attention. Life was supposed to be stingy with its secrets, well what better place to hide them, not in some remote place but in plain view where nobody would think to look.

He smiled at its directness, but underneath he could feel the fear. You couldn't get lost in trying to find it or trying to avoid it, it was always right in front of you waiting for you to sit down face to face. He thought of himself at thirteen innocently searching for God and it turned out his greatest fear was he was everywhere, and you had to come to terms.

The radio station where he was co-host was in downtown Philadelphia. Michael came up hurriedly favoring his right leg, while balancing coffee and a well worn shoulder briefcase. As Michael passed the staff members he heard the intro to the show.

"From the city of brotherly love, welcome to Inside America, where you the listener help uncover the truth." Sara Ellison was seated in front of a microphone with headphones on. To her right a computer screen revealed caller information.

"I'm Sara Ellison, with Michael Flaherty, former DEA agent and now a private security consultant. We're talking about the brutal killing of an FBI undercover agent, allegedly by the militia."

Michael entered and as he put on headphones, Sara handed him papers to read. He was impressed with what he saw. He gave her a thumbs up as she continued.

"Joe in Lansing Michigan, you're on the air."

"Sara, who are you trying to be, the liberal Rush Limbaugh? Allegedly?! The militia aren't patriots, they're criminals. Hell with the FBI, we should send in the army. And if this President won't do it, we'll get one who will!"

"Right. Imagine how much we'll save on court costs and haggling over that silly bill of rights. Kathy from Corvallis, Oregon."

"Michael, long time listener, even before you became a regular. The government betrayed you. Weren't you the one who called your superiors traitors? You should be a friend of the militia."

"I did say that," Michael replied, his mind still on Sara's papers. "Those are harsh words, but I'll stand by them. But the government didn't betray me, certain people in the government did. That's an important distinction. We have a country based on law not men, and because particular men-"

The listener cut in. "I know where you're going, but it's more than that. There's a pattern."

Michael searched for the core. "It still comes down to the actions of men. The idea of government is not the problem."

"What about the idea that the government governs best that governs least?" Kathy replied paraphrasing Jefferson.

Michael was still searching. "That's a mighty fine idea Jefferson had and we should keep it always in mind. But when it came down to it when he was President, he governed pretty hot and heavy. Bought the Louisiana purchase."

Sara barely could wait to respond. "I know it's not exactly fashionable, but we need government, lots of it. I know a lot of you feel you never get a real choice, but where else are we going to get democracy. We've got corporations, political interest groups, fundamentalists, extremists. They all have their goals. They may be right or wrong. But one thing's certain. They're sure not going to put it to a vote. Our problem is not the amount of government. Our problem is the lack of democracy."

Sara went back to the phones. "A call from right here in Philadelphia." There was the sound of a hang up as the call got disconnected.

"Whoops, we lost him. On line three, Randy, a militia member from Larkinsville, Alabama."

"We didn't kill anybody, and the government's going to come after us just the same. That's why they want to take away our guns, so they can attack us when they want." Randy's baby cried in the background as he went on. "I prayed for God to show me a way for my family, and he has."

Sara was about to respond when Michael signaled he would take it. He tried to be conciliatory.

"I've documented government abuse. I've also reported on some reckless militia activity. I know there's been a lot of talk, people quoting Jefferson and the tree of liberty, blood of patriots thing. But I think after all these years what impresses us is not the bloodletting of those patriots, but their wisdom and foresight."

"Our local call is back, go ahead line four."

"Sara, good work on exposing the militia. Keep it up. You'll be as dead as that FBI agent!"

Enraged, Michael jumped in. "Don't threaten her, you son of a bitch! Come after me. I'll go one better-"

The sound of the caller hanging up cut Michael off.

Sara masked her fear. "We're off to a lively start. Let's hear from a caller in Sioux City, Iowa."

"You guys make wild claims about the militia, why don't you just name names?"

Sara wanted a moment to cool things off. "We've got a commercial, want to hang on?"

"You're not out of time, you're out of liberal bullshit."

Michael couldn't resist. "You want names?" As Sara silently mouthed the word "No", Michael continued.

"How about Russell Everett for starters. Next week we'll document the right wing organization he works for, and the money trail to the militia and Allan Shaw. So much for all our liberal bullshit.

* * *

The Runway Cafe in a small municipal airport in south-eastern Pennsylvania had been aggressively overdecorated with a vintage aircraft motif down to the glassware and napkins. There was a partial view of the runway through the windows.

Arens entered the restaurant, passing by the bar where the bartender was wiping down the counter. The TV over the bar featured a news segment which captured Arens' attention. A female newscaster was standing in front of a farmhouse, while FBI agents were busy collecting evidence.

"The early morning raid left two militia seriously wounded. The FBI seized automatic weapons, explosives and bomb making materials."

Arens joked to the bartender. "Must have been planning one hell of a hunting trip."

As they continued to talk, Everett was sitting at a booth at the back of the restaurant. He was sipping a drink while he pondered the chances of his current operation.

Richard Coulter had given him an difficult challenge, set the stage for Shaw winning the Presidency. When Everett insisted he needed to choreograph Shaw's every move, Coulter gave him the bad news. It came in triplicate Everett noticed. Shaw was honest and outspoken and his own man.

"That'll get him close to the White House, Arlington Cemetery," Everett commented.

Coulter had shown him a draft of Shaw's upcoming speech. "We're losing the war on drugs, we're losing the war on terror. The only war our government is winning is the war on the American people."

To top it off Shaw had made it clear to Coulter he would only run if he could make good a promise to win those wars. No small challenge.

Everett thought about it in military terms, momentum and leverage. How much leverage could a well financed handful of people exert? Even if he saw to it they were extremely well financed.

He thought of success stories from Joshua to Guatemala to the Bolsheviks. But these were isolated instances in a sea of contrary ones. Most of the time history has a damn stubborn linearity where it takes a damn lot of shovels to move a mountain. But those other times of instability where a butterfly's wings can cause a storm. They keep you coming back.

Easy to say after the fact that the time had arrived for this idea or that movement, but how to know this from the inside as it happens. That would be a dream. A perfect tactician, in touch with the grain of history and able to read its fault lines like a diamond cutter. He was speculating that it required some impossible combination of sensitivity and aggression as Arens approached his table.

Arens noticed Everett deep in thought and his orange juice and vodka drink. "Philosophizing with a screwdriver?"

"No, I leave that to you. I'm a practical sort." Everett was straight-faced, apparently missing Arens' wit.

"Just a joke about my favorite philosopher," Arens started to explain before he realized that Everett was putting him on.

"You had me for a moment. Practical sort."

Everett pulled out two envelopes and slid them across the table. Arens examined one. It was filled with new $100 bills. Inside the other was a promotional photo of Michael and Sara. Arens viewed it with an intensity that ensured they were two faces he would never forget. "Rumor is you know this guy."

"It was nothing personal. Neither is this."

"Sure, just a couple of knights in shining armor. You know you're an artifact."

"Undoubtedly."

"No, seriously," Arens said pushing his point. "That's why I like you. It's a new day. Everything is up for grabs, loyalty is out the window. You and this guy Flaherty are relics. Nations are obsolete which leaves you patriots without a country. The difference between you and this guy is you know it, and still you choose to sign on. In Japan they'd consider you a National Treasure."

"Remind me to have myself registered," Everett responded dismissively.

Arens pointed to the photos. "What do these two know?"

"If they're not guessing it could mean a problem."

"You want a solution?"

"I want to know how they know. That's just as important as what they know."

As Everett lit up a cigarette with a restaurant matchbook he asked Arens, "If everything's up for grabs what about you?"

"I refuse to bow to the limitations of my time. History is not on your side old buddy. But I'm a romantic, I still like the odds."

Everett couldn't resist a smile.

* * *

Michael and Sara made it a habit to meet once a week at an upscale bar near the studio to casually talk over how the show was going. Their meeting now was not casual. Michael and Sara were both drinking, Michael in earnest. Sara was pressing a heated argument. "Two years, and in thirty seconds you blew it. If it turns out to be Everett, and that's a big if, I don't want it to look like you are just getting even."

Angry himself, Michael tried to lower the volume. "Nothing's blown. You're just sore because I was the one that went with your information."

"I'm not sore or jealous, I'm awake. There are people out there who'd like nothing better than make us look ridiculous."

"You're not giving me any credit for some sense. You know I wouldn't have gone with it if it didn't look good. You saw it."

"Okay it looked good. Maybe it's too good. Why couldn't it be a plant? After all it was an anonymous source, two mailings a week apart."

Michael was incensed. "Great, we'll just wait till hell freezes to go at Everett." He looked around for a waitress. He caught her eye and signaled more of the same for the two of them.

Sara had had enough, both drink and his questioning. She said sharply, "You don't trust me, do you?"

"I know about trust. I believed people when they said 'till death due us part' and 'we're going to win the war on drugs'. But trust loses to secret agendas. The government, people against the government, the DEA."

"So what's my secret agenda?" Sara challenged.

"To show up your ex husband, piss off your rich relatives, be famous, I don't know."

Hurt, Sara shifted gears. "What I know is that you poured gasoline on a fire because the only thing that matters to you is get Everett at any cost."

Michael sensed the fear under Sara's brave front. "That guy tonight is an impotent little man who calls in so he can feel powerful."

"And if you're wrong?"

"I could stay at the house?"

"I think we've got enough to handle with our relationship backed off to where it is."

The waitress arrived with the drinks and Michael paid her. She smiled at him as she left and he avoided the temptation to smile back.

Sara and Michael resumed their argument with a fading sense of resolution. Michael went first.

"You put my side of the story on the air, and I owe you. But there's too much at stake."

"I gather you don't like my standards," Sara said, still hoping Michael would somehow deny it. He might have been able to if his emotions hadn't been in free fall.

Sara angrily crossed the Rubicon. "Maybe you should quit."

Michael abruptly got up. "I already have, you just didn't notice. Thanks for the CDs. I'll see you around." In a fury he downed his drink and then Sara's and walked away.

* * *

Israeli Intelligence following the itinerary of key Middle Eastern figures became aware of their intersection with Everett's trip to Salzburg. Based on the work of informants and double agents the Mossad determined that this secret meeting involved an arms deal of a moderately significant nature. The usual force of a hierarchical bureaucracy made this point of view almost universally held. A dissenting Officer's challenge went unheeded. Eilat Harel was after all an Algerian Jew in an Ashkenazi universe.

Shy and unimposing physically, Harel's skills at violence were astonishingly quick and lethal. Shortly after he had emigrated to Israel from France he nearly killed one of the Mossad's top agents in a bar dispute. It was either arrest him or hire him, and the Mossad chose the latter.

In the beginning they had seen him only as a possible assassin, or low grade operative in North Africa. Increasingly they became aware of his shrewd tactical sense acquired during his youth in the slums of Algeria and France.

He finally convinced his superior that his doubts about the official story were worth looking into. Assets in America were contacted and asked to verify Everett's intentions.

CHAPTER 9

Just pick your poison and we'll swim in it

A cab slowly made its way through the night traffic of New Orleans' French Quarter. Two men were in the backseat. They looked out of the same window at the passing scene, but it was a different world each of them saw. One coolly abstracted the city, taking what he wanted and discarding the rest, reshaping it to his liking with emphatic yeses and nos. Cajun not Creole. Funerals and history and politics, not Mardi Gras and Dixieland.

The other man thought no was an unpleasant, silly word. Time was like a heavy handed manic sculptor that reduced everything smaller than the Grand Tetons to furrows and dust. Might as well enjoy it all while you can.

Everett was holding an attache case. Next to Everett was Dan Hollings. The two men had similar medium build, but while Everett was contained, almost at attention in his, Hollings seemed to overflow its boundaries, definitely at ease. In his 40's and a native of New Orleans, Hollings only concession to a crisp line was the cut of his expensive suit.

"I feel like I'm with a legend, Colonel. I can call you Colonel, even though you're retired?"

"Whatever is simplest."

"I've been looking forward to this. It's not often I get an opportunity to meet someone who helped win the cold war. It's a little awkward, but I guess I'll just say thanks."

"I appreciate that Dan. I wish I could tell you we lived happily ever after. But that's for fairy tales. Unfortunately we've got serious problems. Dan, I was hoping you could show these reports to Congressman Shaw."

Everett handed the attache case to Hollings. Hollings took it with a smile, trying not to show his concern that Everett had revealed at least part of its contents to him. It's true that he was Shaw's trusted aide, they went back forever, but he had expected Everett to have him just act as a courier. That's the way they do these things, unless. He didn't want to pursue unless.

"Colonel, if this biological stuff can really do what they say, why hasn't anybody used it?"

"It's been turned down by every administration since the prototype was offered to Jimmy Carter."

"You're not answering my question."

"We're talking about a five hundred billion dollar a year business. That's enough money to buy governments, even ours. You have no idea. Dan, you have any experience with the Mafia?"

"I'm from New Orleans, Colonel," Hollings replied knowingly.

"A President's life would be in constant jeopardy."

"I know Allan, that's not going to frighten him off."

"That's why I'm here."

The Cab pulled up to a five star hotel. The two got out, and Hollings checked his watch and looked around. Tess Prud- homme was walking toward him. In her twenties, she had styled red hair and was wearing a sheath dress, a single strand of pearls and a broad brimmed hat.

Hollings enjoyed his initial take on her. An attractive young socialite who had escaped a boring luncheon and was trying to find something declassé to amuse herself. The assur- ance of her carriage and movement was only slightly modified by the fact that she was quite drunk.

"Ted??"

"Ted Gilbert, pride of Jefferson parish. And you must be?"

"Diane. Sorry I'm late."

Tess' eye contact was disturbingly penetrating, but also so inviting that Hollings didn't mind the intrusion.

"You're worth waiting for. Diane this is..." Everett clearly didn't want to be introduced.

"... a friend, who unfortunately has a prior engagement."

"Too bad, he's cute."

Tess started to shake hands with a reluctant Everett, but instead embraced him. She ran her hand teasingly below his waist.

"Sure I can't change your mind?"

"That's not my mind."

Hollings took Tess in one arm, and the attache case in the

other. Everett returned to the cab which pulled out into traffic. Hollings walked Tess toward the hotel entrance. "Now let's see if everything comes to those who wait."

The two were alone as the hotel elevator took them up to their room. Hollings was a little nervous as he couldn't help but notice that Tess' drunken behavior while sexy and funny, had a an edginess. "It's too bad your friend couldn't join us. Where's his team spirit? What does he do, he's so busy?"

Hollings tried to be casual in his response. "He's a business-man like me."

"He's no businessman, I know exactly what he is."

"What's that?" Hollings asked a little nervously.

"Let's have a little bet I get it. I'm good at this. I know my johns."

"What's the stakes?" Hollings asked with faked enthusiasm.

"Double or nothing. I win I get twice my usual, I lose I do you gratis."

Hollings was a born gambler. "You're on."

"He's a scientist," Tess said confidently.

"That's amazing," Hollings replied with relief. "I owe you."

"See I told you I was good."

"No doubt about it."

"I've got another bet. We'll make it higher odds this time."

Hollings wasn't thrilled.

"I bet you're lying. And I bet I can tell you why."

Hollings stared at her in disbelief.

"How about it?" Tess urged.

Hollings was in a cold sweat. Tess gave him a sweet smile.

"Don't worry, it's just a little game. Making you sweat a little makes the sex that much hotter." Hollings wasn't quite convinced. Tess went on as the elevator stopped. "Everybody's got something to hide. The trick is knowing they'll pay double to cover for it."

Inside the hotel room Hollings set the attache case on the dresser and paid a bellhop at the door. Tess opened a bottle of champagne and began drinking it straight from the bottle.

"Great vintage."

"It's been a while since I've done this," Hollings said very unconvincingly.

"I've been busy with choir practice myself. Just pick your poison and we'll swim in it."

Hollings looked at her to see if she was serious. It was a nice image even if she wasn't, but she was. He let the image entertain him as he saw himself picking out a bottle in a sort of pharmacy of ecstasy, a cross between a Chinese herb store and a border town farmacia. He was experienced with such choices and knew that like in Alice in Wonderland some would make you larger and some would make you smaller. He couldn't decide which this would make him, so he chose to make her smaller.

"I have a thing about the Civil War, let's talk about Longstreet."

"You serious or you just into humiliating dumb hookers?"

Tess went on before Hollings had a chance to answer. "Talking about Longstreet will be $150 extra. Pretending I don't know will be $300 extra." Hollings was both intrigued and put off. Tess picked it up. "You feel uncomfortable there's more to me. You could have played it safe, you're the type that's got connections, why pick me off the street?"

"Let's just say I like taking chances. Maybe you come up with something different. Dumb is okay, but come to think of it maybe I'd like them hot at both ends if they came that way, but it never works like that."

"You don't work like that. Too dangerous. Men prefer the danger of death and killing. War and all that. Don't you think?"

"I guess it goes with the territory," Hollings said with uncertainty.

"But killing is woman's work too." Tess formed her fingers into a mock gun and pointed them at Hollings' head. "I'm good at it. Men ask me to do it for them all the time. Maybe there's something you'd like killed. Tess moved toward Hollings firing off her "gun" as she went on. "I kill loneliness, I kill emptiness, I kill boredom, I kill fear. What do you have that's deep and dark you want killed?"

Hollings had regained his composure. "I'm in a peace loving kind of mood. Tonight I'm just into watching."

Tess shook her head in mock disapproval. "You and everybody else. What's happening to this country? There's a TV over there," Tess gestured. Hollings looked disappointed. Tess flashed a smile. "I was just kidding. I'll give you something to watch. Check the southern exposure."

Tess turned around and tantalizingly lifted her dress. Hollings appreciated that she was naked underneath it, appreciated that her body required no window dressing. She did a slow grind against the dresser.

"Or maybe you like little schoolgirls?"

Tess plopped herself down in a chair, her legs straddling the arms. She coyly started playing with herself, moaning breathlessly. She suddenly stopped and walked over to Hollings who was mesmerized.

"But I'm tired of all this watching. Aren't you? We should get close. Rub each other the wrong way, the right way, every way." Tess took a guzzle of champagne. "Come on now, there must be a real man inside you somewhere. Show me you've got something more than a pair of eyes."

Hollings began passionately kissing her. Tess pulled away. "How romantic. You're the kind that gives flowers and then can't even get it up."

Tess reached for his crotch. "You're as soft as a baby's ass," Tess taunted. "You queer or something."

Hollings snapped. "Fucking whore!" In a rage Hollings ripped open Tess' dress. He shoved her up against a wall, slapping her across the face. Blood gushed out of her mouth. Wincing in pain, she pulled away from him.

"You've broken my fucking nose! Get me a towel. Hurry!"

Hollings hesitated, weighing passion against propriety as he caught his breath. Tess tried to staunch the bleeding with her hand.

"If you like it we'll continue, but it's blood on a towel or your new suit."

"I definitely like it," Hollings said as he turned and went into the bathroom. In an instant Tess turned cold sober. She spit the remains of a prop blood pill from her mouth.

Hollings finished wetting a towel in the sink and came back into the bedroom. He was stunned to see the room was empty and the door wide open. A moment later he realized the attache case was gone.

Swearing a blue streak, he dashed into the hallway and ran into a Japanese bellhop who was carrying a tray filled with pastries and coffee. As they untangled, Tess hurried down the hotel stairwell with the attache case. She paused to see if there was anyone following her.

There was an artist's portfolio case on the landing. She placed the attache case inside of it. She took a nylon coat out of her purse and put it on, wiped the fake blood from her mouth and removed her wig. A pair of sunglasses and a beret over her blonde hair finished her transformation.

Moments later Tess emerged from the hotel side entrance. She walked casually away and got into a cab. She had the cabby drive around until she was satisfied she wasn't being followed. She picked up her car and drove to her apartment.

As Tess neared her door she heard one of her Edith Piaf CDs playing inside. She loved that Kit shared her taste. She expected to see him when she walked in, but the apartment was completely dark. She was shocked to hear Hollings' voice.

"Nice music, now give me back my case, and nobody gets hurt."

Panicked, Tess dropped the portfolio case. She was about to bolt out the door when she heard the sound of laughter. The light went on and she saw the bellhop, Kit Hamada, laughing at his practical joke.

Kit was in his late twenties and pleased that his "too pretty" looks which had mocked the severity of his background, finally were being replaced by well worn character. Like all self made men, he had some help.

He got his nickname Kit from his favorite writer, Kita Ikki, his vintage clothes from the top designers, his missing finger tip from the Japanese mafia and his right wing dreams from the best minds of Japan's history.

Kit's laughter stopped abruptly as he noticed Tess' bruised face. "I wish you didn't play it so full out." He started to get ice out of the refrigerator.

"Don't bother, I'm used to it. "

Kit gave Tess a questioning look. She shrugged it off. "I like to prove I'm up to taking what life has to offer." Tess laughed to herself. A lifetime of pain echoed in it.

"You sure you weren't followed?"

"Positive."

Kit gently applied the ice to Tess' face as she winced. "I can't stand watching this happen to you."

Tess wasn't about to be moved by his concern. "Florence Nightingale, let's get to business."

She got the attache case out of the portfolio and handed it to Kit.

"Our usual bet on what goodies are inside," Kit offered as he placed it on the kitchen table.

"I've had enough betting for the evening."

"Maybe we got something. The guy went crazy." Kit

imitated Hollings squawking. They both laughed as he took out a small tool and expertly snapped the lock, adding, "Just so it's better than last time."

Kit opened the case. He and Tess saw file folders sitting on top of a bed of $100 bills. They both were speechless until Kit spoke up. "Not exactly an Italian sausage sandwich and a change of underwear."

"We've bought trouble," Tess said as she set the file folders aside and looked at the bills.

"Funny?" Kit asked hopefully.

"Coin of the realm."

Kit sized it up. "About three hundred thousand." He started to look over the papers.

"What have we got?" Tess asked.

Kit stopped reading. "I'm not sure. We're definitely in somebody else's wet dream."

"I have a feeling we'll be asked to leave."

"With a vengeance."

"I better find out what we've inherited," Tess said as she refilled the attache case and prepared to go.

"Be careful," Kit warned with more concern than was comfortable. "Or he'll short you," he added with a forced smile.

Tess left the building. She surveyed the street. Too many unfamiliar faces, so she just had to have faith she had gotten away clean. She hurried to her car, started driving, checking behind her. Nobody was following. She picked up her cell. The traffic noise meant she didn't have to be subtle.

"I don't give a shit you said don't call here. Yeah, I got it.

Easy payback, you said. So I looked. It's a goddamn good thing I did. All the sudden I'm in the middle of some war. Bullshit it isn't. Then what is it? It is my business. It's my ass, it's my business. I don't want to be protected. I don't want to need to be protected. Just tell me whose money this is. Fuck you."

Tess abruptly ended the call. She thought it over. Her second call was routed to a number in western Massachusetts.

* * *

Left alone, Kit made himself some coffee and sat down to wait for Tess to return. As he did so, he tried to remember as much of the papers as he could. They were about drugs, and he had heard that his former "friends" in the Yakuza, the Japanese mafia, were looking for something like this.

A European dealer in technological secrets had contacted them. He claimed he had some scientific information crucial to their drug trade that he wanted to exchange for money. The asking price put them off, but also made them curious. He only told them it was American and stolen and they would understand when they saw it. They never got the chance. He never showed up for the meeting.

Their first response was it was a scam and he had lost his nerve. But soon the rumor began to circulate that he was bumped off by American intelligence.

Now here were scientific papers about drugs and an attache case filled with money. It could be what they were after. That would more than settle an old debt he had with them.

He remembered with some pain how he had wanted to join

the Yakuza because they had a code of honor. It was youthful folly to think so. The only code left worthy of mention in Japan was the serial number on the yen note. He was reflecting on what it would take to revive an ancient tradition when he heard someone at the front door. Tess has come back he thought as it opened.

* * *

Hollings got a message to Everett right after the attache case was stolen. He was advised what to say if he were contacted by the police. He couldn't believe Everett wanted to reveal as much as he did so he asked him to repeat his instructions.

Three days later the New Orleans FBI got a tip from an informant about the robbery and called Hollings. He didn't like it. It was a direct call and the agent wasn't his usual contact. Holllings made it clear he would only speak to his contact and hung up. When they met Hollings was furious.

"Why don't you just put a photo of us on Facebook?"

"Sorry. Someone in the office just got overheated when they got a tip it was a lot of money and drug related."

"The only drugs involved are the ones your agent is on."

"So what is involved?"

Hollings described the robbery and the attache case filled with money, leaving out Everett and the papers. The agent assumed a tone as if they had been friends since they wore diapers.

"Give me a little something to feed the folks in Washington

and we'll all be happy."

Hollings knew to hesitate. "It was campaign money."

"Shaw's?"

Hollings nodded.

"Who's the rich uncle?"

"An Italian friend of ours," Hollings lied.

The agent smiled. "Well if Washington asks, I'll tell them I'm working on it."

Hollings smiled back, but he was thinking about Everett. Everett was feeding the FBI a mixture of truth and lies. He didn't have to give them either.

CHAPTER 10

Gauguin's questions

Sara's house was in an upscale suburb of Philadelphia. Unlike the other houses on her block, Sara's front yard was filled with children's toys. Today was her daughter's birthday, but the yard was always like that. Sara was in the playroom finishing decorating as she waited for the guests to arrive. Jack was in the living room with four year old Melanie, while seven year old Jason was loudly strafing presents with his hand.

"I want to open a present," Melanie more than urged.

"Wouldn't it be more fun if we waited until everybody was here?" Jack reasoned.

Melanie shook her head. Tommy's strafing had gone up some decibels. Jack addressed it.

"Tom, could we tone down World War Three?" Tommy was in a world of his own. Jack turned back to Melanie. "Okay. How about as a favor to me?" Melanie shook her head.

"Good. I'm glad that's settled," Jack said with joking finality as Sara walked into the room. She was obviously angry with him and he noticed with concern.

Outside dark clouds were framed in light by the sun. Michael didn't notice as he sped through the curves on the road that led to Sara's. A birthday present was on the seat next to him. He needed some counterpoint to his anxious thoughts about reconnecting with Sara. He reached into the glove compartment for a CD and started it.

"I've called this talk Gauguin's Questions, which refers to the title of one of his paintings. He painted it in 1897 in Tahiti. If you're ever get a chance to visit the Fine Arts Museum in Boston you should definitely do so. It's on display there and a masterpiece and a summing up of his art. Its title is, 'Where do we come from?, Who are we?, Where are we going?'

"In all of Gauguin's travels, from Europe to the South Seas, you can sense he's searching for an interaction with people and place that would put him in touch with the source of his creativity. I think in doing so he was trying to find answers to those three questions.

"Which brings us to our sprees, our addictions and our fantasies. I think these are attempts to answer these same three questions: Where do we come from?, Who are we?, Where are we going?"

"Where are we going?" Michael repeated to himself as the CD continued. "We're going to a birthday party. My son's birthday is...What the hell why dwell? Get off it. Sara invited you, she wants to make up."

Across the highway was a produce stand with a United Parcel truck parked nearby. Michael glanced over. The truck was empty, and no one was working the fruit stand. Michael puzzled over the oddity. He looked for someone in the surrounding trees.

"When you got to go, you got to go," he said to himself as if to test out a theory. He drove on with a look on his face as though it didn't pass muster.

Jack entered the kitchen as Sara was making dip in a food processor. She wasn't happy. Jack tried to make peace. "It's Melanie's birthday, can we just forget it?"

"You always want to forget it when you're wrong."

"Okay, a terrible thing happened to Michael. But that was years ago. He's got no friends, he barely keeps his business afloat, he drove his own family away. His ex won't even let him see his son."

"You're condemning him for her being unforgiving."

"All I know is Michael has no life, and you do."

"He has a life. For once you could try to appreciate what he's trying to do."

"You don't appreciate what I'm trying to do. It's time to move on. You've got the talent for something better."

"Better or less threatening?"

"It is threatening when it ends up with some moron calling like that. Look, it's not a matter of blaming anybody. I had no idea myself it would-"

One of the parents swung open the kitchen door. "We're about ready."

In the living room Michael was talking to the two kids. Melanie was holding a large plainly wrapped present. "Are you going to open it?" Michael asked.

"Jason's lost the card," Melanie said accusingly.

Jason defended himself. "Shows what you know. It didn't have a card. The deliveryman gave it to Mommy. And now it's... mine."

Jason snatched the present and ran toward the backyard with Melanie in screaming pursuit. Jack went after them. Michael looked like he'd put two and two together and didn't like the answer.

Melanie chased Jason around a jungle gym as he teased her with the present. Jason tripped and fell, but landed on his back still holding the package to his chest. The two tussled for it. It was about to fall as Jack came up and caught it.

"Jason stop teasing Melanie. It's her birthday and it's her present. Understand."

"Then why can't I open it?" Melanie reasoned.

Jack was about to argue, but the logic got him. "Okay, just this one present."

Melanie was thrilled. She immediately began undoing the ribbon and peeling away the wrapping paper.

"Don't open it!," Michael yelled.

Jack looked up and saw Michael running toward him shouting. Melanie tore away the paper and started to lift the lid off the box. Jack suddenly held the lid closed as Michael ran up with Sara behind him.

"What the hell is going on?" Jack demanded.

"I think it's a bomb. Set it down easy and get away from it."

"Bomb?!" Jack said in disbelief. "What are you talking-"

Michael didn't let him finish."We're wasting time."

Sara tried to reason with Michael. "Michael, I don't think the gift-"

Michael grabbed the package out of Jack's hands and heaved it. The package tumbled through the air, finally hitting the ground between some trees. The group watched the package in stunned silence. Michael braced for an explosion. A moment passed. Another. No explosion. Just silence. Melanie started to cry, breaking the silence.

"This is absolutely crazy," Jack said as he started walking toward the package.

"It could still go off," Michael warned.

Jack didn't stop. Michael pulled out a gun and ordered Jack to stop.

"This is madness," Sara said frantically.

Jack kept going. Michael raised his gun and fired. The package jumped as a bullet went through it. No explosion. Jack was stunned, while the children cried even louder.

Michael fired again. The package jumped again. Again nothing. Michael fired again and again and again. Nothing happened. The children were hysterical. Jack, absolutely furious, turned to Sara.

"This is the insanity your show is leading to. Ex DEA nut shoots birthday present."

Jack turned and walked angrily into the house. Furious herself, Sara comforted her children as she led them inside. Michael was left standing alone.

CHAPTER 11

Process of elimination. That's our specialty.

The three were waiting for a call. Tony, Gino and Pasquale. They were sitting around a motel room in Oakland waiting to kill someone. Instead they were killing time playing cards and watching television. Perhaps exacting dull revenge on time that would kill them. Gino was the only one amused by the documentary on organized crime on the TV. Tony finally had more than his fill.

"Can it."

"It's like home movies," Gino said pleading his case. Pasquale gestured dismissively toward the TV.

"Organized crime. They're dreaming. Frankie's so organized he needs a compass to find his dick."

Tony's cell vibrated and he answered it. He had a brief conversation and returned to the table.

"She's the one."

"What about the others?" Pasquale asked.

Tony shook his head. "She was the only one that fit. They said it was a process of elimination."

Gino lit up as if he had won the lottery. "Process of elimina-tion. That's our specialty." They all laughed. They left the motel and drove to her house in Oakland. They were in good spirits. This was a night on the town. The only real danger they all agreed was the shitty neighborhood. She had a regular sched-ule and they waited.

It got late and cold. Their humor changed. She didn't come home. They made jokes about her sexual preferences.

They tried the next day, but Rehema was out of town and stayed that way. Everett was taking no chances. He was moni-toring the mob's wiretapped conversations through contacts he had in the government.

* * *

George Hilliard's family was wealthy. His mother was one of the major black fund-raisers for the Republican party. She had savvy and clout. Hilliard had distanced himself from his family to make his own way in the DEA. But if he had to fall along with Michael and the other agent, she made sure his descent was upwards to the Washington office of the FBI.

She saw a future in politics for him. His record as an administrator was not stellar, but with his connections he proved invaluable when he was taken on as a political liaison in the White House staff.

With an election coming up there were points to be scored passing along any relevant information. A paper crossed his desk about a robbery of Allan Shaw's assistant and campaign money and the Mafia.

Hilliard began confirming the report. It was a career builder and he wanted to get it right.

Prints were taken off of a handcart. Finding no match in the US, the FBI went international. The Japanese police identified the man as Masao "Kit" Hamada . He was wanted in Japan in connection with his involvement in the Yakuza. Someone in the National Police Agency also provided the Yakuza with details of the robbery.

CHAPTER 12

Like letting whores in a church

Michael's week was an agony. He had humiliated himself and his self recriminations were only partially relieved by filling the days with his security business. He almost made it through without anybody noticing he didn't have the slightest interest in what he was doing, only in something that would take the edge off the replays of the events at Sara's.

He was trying to be all business as he was installing a security system for a voluptuous middle aged woman. She had dyed black hair and a nonstop enthusiasm for rings and her start up venture involving a new miracle anti-aging cream. Between her heady perfume, inviting smile and the uncooperative wiring he was on overload as he listened to her sales pitch.

"All the jet setters had to go to Europe to get it, it was so rare. The secret ingredient was placenta of some mountain goat, like there were five in the whole wide world. A thousand dollars an ounce they charged for it. And you know what the miracle is?"

Michael barely had time to shake his head as she was traveling on. "They don't need the goat any more. Can you believe that?" Michael was ready to believe anything. He tried desperately to focus on the wiring as she proclaimed the wonders of a Swiss pharmaceutical company, Zardoz she thought it was called, and how it could make the stuff from scratch like mother's chocolate cake. "Well not my mother, she made it from mix but you get the idea."

Michael was finishing up as she got to the clincher. "You think it works?" she said modeling her face and arms that mimicked white jade and fine porcelain.

"Definitely," Michael replied without having to lie. She already had her answer from the way he looked at her.

"You ever mix business with pleasure."

"Only at my worst."

"Leave it to me to bring out the worst in a guy," she added, half disappointed and half still trying.

"The best and the worst both," Michael started to say with frustrated intensity. He could see it was too much. He quietly explained. "It's not that I'm uninterested. I'm too interested.

He sat in his car getting himself together. He noticed he was sweating. "The strain of restraint," he muttered to himself. He said it again. It was a favorite phrase. It summed up. He went home and listened to his answering machine. "This is United Parcel. We did have a delivery in your general area yesterday. Hope that clears everything up."

"Oh yeah," he said to himself. "Like this is going to do." Michael poured himself a large drink. Several large drinks later he had the "clarity" he was looking for. Unfortunately, it was accompanied, as it often was, by an unruly inner dialogue.

Losing it. Shooting a gun with kids around. Am I losing it or already lost it. Five shots into that damn package, I'm thorough I'll say that. Today, got through today, didn't make a complete fool of myself. Can't believe my instincts are that off.

In excruciating detail he remembered the radio show, Sara's outburst, the parcel truck, the party, the package, the gun. He replayed the sequence over and over as if doing so were going to wear out the links in the chain of events and free them from their inevitable conclusion.

He finally caught a glimpse of himself on the not so merry go round. Time to switch channels, fill his head with something else. He picked out a jazz CD. He started to replace the CD already in the player when he noticed it was one of Nime's CDs.

He thought of Sara. In a mix of emotions,the one that won out was one of the more painful, how she had tried to help him. He owed her, that's what he had said. Well listening to the damn CD was one of the easier ways to pay off some of that debt.

Michael noticed the title, "Gauguin's Questions #3" as he put the CD back in the machine. "Let's see how Gauguin the Third mixes with a Black Russian." He poured himself another drink.

"We began last time with Gauguin's questions. 'Where do we come from?, Who are we?, Where are we gong?' Now we'll turn to fantasy and see how it helps us with these questions.

"It's interesting how we don't we allow ourselves both

excitement and meaning. What would happen if our hearts, minds and genitals were all moved? It's our birthright to be totally present, totally whole.

"We have a morbid fear of the complete person. Divide and conquer is not only a time honored strategy in the political sphere. On a personal level we have been divided and conquered and now we continue the job ourselves. We have been set off from ourselves, against ourselves.

"Here we lost the ability to speak forthrightly, here we lost some hope, here we lost some trust in others, her we lost some faith in our strength, our feeling of being beautiful, here we forgot how to dance. It definitely diminishes us, but makes us more manageable. The political implications of this I'll save for another talk. Right now I'd like to move on to Gauguin's third question, 'Where are we going?'

"The people that are going to help us answer that question are the people in your fantasies.

"Since fantasy is about arousal, it involves exciting ourselves. You can't tell yourself to get sexually excited the same way you tell yourself to move your arm. We have to communicate with the source of our ecstasy. And the figures of fantasy are how we do it.

"We'll try to talk to them directly and see what they have to tell us. I'm sure you're saying to yourself, what possibly could they have to tell me, they're just something I made up.

"First of all I'd say that they're not just something that you made up. Who they are and the roles they play reflect your personal history. Through them you connect to the most exciting, vital depths of your being. That puts them in a privileged position to be witnesses to your inner life.

"Rather than having nothing to tell us, they have so much to reveal we'd rather have them play out their usual roles. That way we are convinced we're just having a good time and nothing more.

"So how to begin this remarkable conversation? What sort of questions do we ask? I mean these people are so extraordinary, so intimate and yet they are strangers to us. They remind us of how much of what we are and what we can be is astonishingly foreign to us.

"And how do they answer? Through your imagination. I think you'll be surprised at what your imagination comes up with, how real and meaningful their response is.

"You can begin by asking them basic questions. Who are you? The answer to this question in itself can be surprising and very revealing. It can give the first clues that the person you're addressing has much more depth than you expected.

"It can also give you a feeling for what further questions you'd like to ask. Do you have something to tell me? Why do you excite me? Why are you in my life? Do you have to something to say about who I am.

"This has all the awkwardness of a first date, which it is in a way. To the degree we all don't know ourselves, a blind date at that."

Michael was thinking about the CD as it went on. He thought about facing these images so casually created, about speaking to them and letting them speak back. The imagined conversation seemed to take place where there never had been a visitor let alone a conversation. Letting them in was like letting whores into a church, and what was more difficult was finding a church inside of them. Something lost in him was in their voices, did he want to hear it?

He emerged from his speculation with a laugh as a phrase from earlier in the day suddenly popped into his head. "They don't need the goat." "They don't need the goat," he said to himself again in amusement. For a moment the phrase lingered as if it had more to offer and then again it was just funny.

CHAPTER 13

Union without consent is rape

Emiliano Diaz was at the mountain resort buried in mud. He was talking to himself as much as to the physical therapist who was working on him. She worked marvels, but was also a notorious gossip. Diaz appreciated both. The new leaders paid little attention to him face to face, but treated what they heard secondhand like gold.

"No, I believe you see an energy in the mud, and that's what helps the arthritis. I say it's like being buried before you're buried. I think that's what does it. Your body gets a taste of that and it shapes up."

The two shared a laugh. Diaz changed the subject, knowing she would repeat every word.

"I hear the fools that are sitting in my chair say I don't know what's going on. They say the Americans are considering attacking us. I am told about it but not asked what to do."

"It's right I'm old. I'm too old. You're always too young and then you're too old. They're all panicked. Idiots. They'll just make matters worse with their revenge.

"It doesn't matter I told them. It's a piece of paper. It'll come to nothing. The politicians aren't going to destroy all this wealth. The biggest business in the world. They don't own it, but it's there when they want to put their hands in.

"A few high minded people. Fools. They think they'll rid the world of evil. They'll get rid of a little evil and replace it with a bigger one. It's nature. Nothing disappears unless there's a substitute. And there's no substitute, believe me."

* * *

"Union without consent is rape" the bumper sticker read. It was on the back of an old Chevy pickup that was sitting in front of a small wood frame house in Larkinsville, Alabama. Fishing gear, including a tackle box were in the bed of the truck. Earl Tolliver was behind the wheel, dressed in jeans and a flannel shirt.

He puffed on a cigarette and tapped nervously to country music coming from the radio. He pulled a pint of whiskey out of the glove box which also contained a gun. He took a long swig from the bottle as he waited for his friend.

Inside the house, a small room off the kitchen had been set aside as a study. It was filled with books, most of them about American history. Randy Hastings was sitting at his desk finishing a letter. It was addressed to his wife and children, but a good deal of it outlined his political philosophy.

Starting with the Declaration of Independence and its statement that government should exist only by "consent of the governed", he documented the ever increasing usurpation of power by the Federal government. The critical act in this continuing outrage was Lincoln's war against the South which completely undermined the right of voluntary association as the basis of government.

To government's "war on its own people" there was finally only one response possible. The response of the founding fathers. Rebellion. It was an action not desired, but forced on the people from Shay's rebellion to the present.

Earl watched as Randy exited his house and walked toward the truck. He was wearing a down vest and carrying a fishing pole. Earl turned off the radio and gestured to Randy.

"Hey boy, did you forget your 'tackle box'?"

Randy hurriedly headed back to the house. Earl took more swigs of whiskey. Randy returned, put the 'tackle box' in the bed of the truck and got in. He was struggling with something and showed it.

"You want to go fishing or what?" Earl chided.

"Sorry. Hard saying good-bye. First time I ever lied to them."

"You'll set it straight. We're coming back heroes."

"I had a dream that told me we weren't coming back."

"Forget it. I don't believe half of the things your crazy head tells you even when you're awake."

Randy's mood didn't change. "I left a letter. Jesus is my witness, I never thought it would come to this."

The truck drove off in the early light.

CHAPTER 14

The Bedroom, the Battlefield, and the Graveyard

Time and drink had taken some of the edge off Michael's agony. But what was allayed in the intensity of his thoughts was made up for by their repetition. No matter what direction his thoughts would go, they'd still dead end in the same place. The backyard with that stupid package.

Prepare for the next show. Think about calling Sara. Think of rechecking the parcel delivery, rechecking the phone call. Think about the information about Everett she had shown him? All Michael's thoughts ended up in the backyard with the package.

He couldn't sleep. What about the therapist's CD? Maybe that would lead somewhere else. He needed a somewhere else. Anything to work on. But what were the people in his fantasies going to say? What if they were silent?

It started to spook him. It was making him feel like he didn't know what was inside his own head. He realized with a laugh nothing new in that. What did he have to lose? And he didn't know the answer to that.

He speculated on a whole variety of their responses, accusatory, funny, hostile, sexy, silent. But speculating wasn't asking. He finally decided to ask. But who shall it be? Why not the girl that started it all. He imagined her sitting across from him. He imagined asking who she was.

She didn't say anything in response, but looked at him as she began to cry. It caught him completely by surprise. It unnerved him like looking in the mirror and seeing a complete stranger. He realized there were tears in his eyes. "I'm coming unglued, this is crazy." He had to stop. But he managed to get some sleep.

The next time he asked, expecting something similar, perhaps hoping for something similar, there were no tears. "Let's just have fun," she said. He asked again. "You don't want to know," she replied. He began to get a queasy feeling.

He summoned up his courage and proceeded. There was a long silence, he was getting nothing and about to give up when suddenly she said "help me". At first quietly and then again and again with more intensity, her voice altering in the process until it seemed it had embodied the voices of all the women in his life.

He stopped, shaken at the realization he had heard his mother's voice. He suddenly remembered a childhood fear that she might be in hell because of what she did. It was an awful, helpless feeling. He didn't need that. He needed a drink and got one. What was the use of this? He couldn't help her. Or his ex wife or Sara or any of the women he imagined he heard. He couldn't save any of them.

At five in the morning he gave up on sleeping and began driving. At first just to be driving and then toward western Massachusetts and Nime's workshop. If Sara had told Nime about her latest revelations Michael wanted to know about it. He saw a hitchhiker and thought about picking her up. He passed her by. He already had more passengers on this trip than he could handle.

* * *

A note left at Sara's box at the station had led to weekly mailings of information. She was naturally skeptical, but it turned out to be interesting material and it kept getting better. It included the revelation about Everett, the militia and Shaw. From its contents she tried to figure out the source. So far her efforts had produced nothing more than whoever it was had very punctual habits as she picked up her mail.

She had made it a habit of putting all important documents from the show in her safety deposit box. She went to her bank with the package. She was friendly with the teller who helped her. When they met they discovered that they were both going through a break up and shared sympathy.

Sara sat down in one of the cubicles. The handwriting on the mailer was familiar. She opened it with expectation and started reading the material.

* * *

Nime had found the small actors' equity theater when he was having his house remodeled and needed another place to give his talks. It was meant to be temporary, but now he wasn't sure. There were two chairs on the stage of the upstairs theater and he was sitting in one of them, talking to a group of people sitting in the audience.

"It's been fitting in a way that we've had a chance to meet here in this theater. We've been working with fantasy, and it's a drama both as an entertainment as well as in its power to reveal the deepest truths about our lives.

"The title of my talk today is 'The Bedroom, the Battlefield and the Graveyard'. They are the site of three great transformative experiences; sex, war and death. We have been focusing on the bedroom and will continue to do so, but I also want to talk about war and death whose meaning is missed.

"The great passions of life have been pushed into some corner and left there. This corner is sex, this corner is war, this corner is death. We want to take sex, war, and death out of the bedroom, battlefield, and graveyard and reclaim those energies for the rest of your life.

"You've probably seen reproductions of the wall paintings in Lascaux, that cave in France. They were done by stone age hunter gatherers twenty five thousand years ago and not only are they exceptionally beautiful, they have a mythic, almost religious significance. They lived in a world where everything had a spirit and they were connected to it all.

"We've severed our connection with it and turned it into something to study and master. In a way you could say we've banished God from Eden. It was the first step in converting Eden and the world into an exploitable resource. The political implications of this we'll save for another time. So how do we reconnect? Make ourselves and the world totally alive.

"Now you may not know it, but you share something in common with Saint Teresa of Avila. You share it with the Sufi mystic Rumi and the alchemist John Dee, court adviser to Queen Elizabeth I. You share it with Maria Sabina, a Mazatec healer and Abraham Abulafia a 13th century Kabbalist. You share it with a shaman whose image was painted on a cave wall 25,000 years ago.

"What do you have in common with all these people? You have been on a quest for a connection that brings insight. Our sprees, addictions and sexual fantasy are in fact vision quests. The only difference is that up to now you have been unaware of it and becoming aware of it will transform your life."

* * *

Michael got to Nime's house by early afternoon. He saw the note posted and found the playhouse in town. He walked upstairs past a sign announcing a production of "Uncle Vanya". He thought to himself it'd be funny if he ended up watching a play. There was a small room that led to the theater. He opened the door and took the first seat he came to.

He was relieved nobody turned around. All eyes were on the stage where Nime and David, a preppy looking, nervous young man were sitting across from one another. Nime was addressing the audience.

Michael sized him up. He had long graying hair. His glasses gave him an intellectual appearance, but his build and physical presence were more like a manual laborer. "No, it's more aggressive than that," Michael thought to himself. He struggled with the image. A high school friend who was on the wrestling team popped into his mind. "Yeah, that's it," Michael concluded. "A wrestler, that's who he reminds me of. Maybe he got that way wrestling with the angels like Jacob."

Satisfied with his take on Nime, Michael shifted his attention to his talk. "I could tell you about it. I could give you an explanation. We do a lot of that, analytic work. And it's very helpful. But in modern life explanation has taken the place of connection. We know more and more of the world, but it doesn't move us.

"So I could tell you that probably this or that happened in your childhood, you had this sort of relationship. But it's like telling you what love is, it's better to experience it. And one way you can do that is through relating to the person in your fantasy. That way you begin to enter into it and it begins to live for you, it begins to move you. Does the world around speak to you, have meaning for you, or is it just stuff out there? So let's continue."

Nime waited as David struggled to say something.

"I just can't talk to him. I worry where he is? Whether he's all right"

"I could tell you that he's all right, that in fact in the most profound way he's still everywhere among us, or that he's in heaven at peace. But this not really about where he is, it's about where you are. And if you can get in touch with that, it would be unnecessary for me to reassure you he's among us or in heaven, you would feel it in a way that nobody could possibly describe."

"I think I get that, but I still..." David's thought drifted off into silence. Nime turned to the audience.

"So we started with David's fantasy encounter with a woman in a deserted office. She's bound and gagged and made love to. And we worked on the fantasy. The woman stepped out of her role and David had a conversation with her and she asked him why he had to tie her up and gag her. And he had no answer. It just brought the conversation to a standstill.

"I suggested he ask himself why he was stuck and it brought up this problem he is having dealing with the death of his brother. And I think if we go into it, we'll see that the woman in David's fantasy is not the only one that's bound and gagged.

"We've talked about war and sex. Death is also one of the areas where we put a lot of our fantasies. It doesn't tell us much about death, but a lot about ourselves. We stick a lot of our fears and energy there. So let's see if we can retrieve some."

Nime turned back to David, but didn't speak right away. Nime sat quietly as if he was listening to the man's silence, and then began again.

"You have visions of your brother being in a dark, empty place somewhere. I can't see this. What I can see is a dark, empty place in you. You're trapped in there somewhere, hold-ing in all your grief, terror, rage and love. Somehow you're going to have to open. Let someone in to that closed space.

"Your brother is dead, we don't know what that means, but we do know what you being dead means. Your brother can't speak to you because you can't speak to him. You would have to connect your voice and your heart and you've choked the life out of both of them. Your brother will live for you when you live."

David began to weep. Michael watched him until suddenly he realized he was holding his breath. He tried to catch it but couldn't. He had to get some air. He hurried down the stairs and outside.

The street was deserted and still. It was if everything were holding its breath. Waiting. Waiting for what? Everything around him seemed to have more of a presence, about to step beyond itself, almost as if it were about to break its inanimate silence and speak.

It lasted for a moment, but it was too much, and then it was gone. A car turned a corner, laughing customers came out of a shop, everything rushed on.

Twenty minutes and a meandering walk later Michael had gained no more composure. There was a pub style bar at the corner and Michael pushed open its carved wood door. He tried to ignore the curious glances the regulars gave him and sat at a table near the exit. There was a large Bass Ale clock behind the bar he promised himself he was going to keep an eye on.

* * *

Sara was lost in thought as she drove her station wagon toward town. As her car headed up a long incline, Sara picked up her cell and messaged Michael without result. She called his landline. The phone rang in his loft. Michael was not there to answer. Sara's voice came over the answering machine.

"Michael, if you're there, pick up. All is forgiven."

Sara was disappointed when she realized Michael wasn't there. "I've got something, but it doesn't quite make sense. Grab some coffee and meet me at the studio! Hurry!"

A mile ahead of Sara a United Parcel truck was idling at the intersection to the highway. A deliveryman with a freckled complexion was at the wheel. He was the Norman Rockwell All-American kid who waved to her outside the radio station. Next to him was a young Latino deliveryman, his hat pulled over his forehead. The driver turned to him.

"Buckle up, Pedro, this is going to be a rough ride."

Pedro seemed unconcerned.

"Suit yourself macho man."

The driver turned left and started down the hill that Sara was going up. The Latino slumped against the door, his head tilted back. His eyes were glazed and there was a bleeding wound on his forehead. He had no need to buckle up, he was dead.

Sara saw the truck coming down the hill on the opposite side of the highway. It suddenly veered to the left heading right at her. She swerved to avoid it.

Two minutes later Sara's car was crumpled against a tree. The United Parcel delivery truck buried in the Volvo's side had a shattered windshield. The Latino was slumped over the steering wheel as though he had been the driver. The other man was gone.

CHAPTER 15

There's no "they"

Every so often Michael would think about the drive back from Massachusetts. At what point was Sara killed? Was there some sign? A sudden twinge in the gut or sweep of emptiness. Maybe if he hadn't stopped at a bar and got plastered there might have been. Instead he was lost in a conversation with himself about his abrupt exit from Nime's workshop.

No medal for that performance. Mister bravery. Now when it comes to facing a gun I stack up pretty good. Maybe because I never had much to lose. But I stack up pretty good. It's the up close and personal. Should be uptight and personal. Next time I'll call ahead and make sure everybody is armed. Next time.

Michael looked up at the Bass Ale clock. It was late. Never too late for this. He added a few more drinks before he drove to his loft. He climbed the stairs unsteadily, but painlessly.

"Great. The only time my knee works is when the rest of me doesn't."

Suddenly Michael noticed his door alarm was turned off. He stared for a second before the thought "it's been disabled" alerted him. He pulled out his gun and started cautiously up the stairs.

He stood to the side of the doorway preparing to rush in. A similar scene flashed through his mind. Gun drawn, Michael was standing outside a warehouse door. He kicked in the door and rushed in.

Blinding light, deafening gunfire and he was on the ground, wounded as three gunmen stood over him. Michael prepared to die. Instead they shot him in the leg. He writhed in pain while his attackers merely laughed.

Michael took a deep breath to block out the memory. He pushed open the door to his loft, expecting gunfire in return. There was none. He entered warily and surveyed the darkened room. Nobody was there.

He turned on the light. He had the strange feeling someone had been there, but the place looked exactly like he had left it. Michael examined the door alarm and realized he forgot to set it. "Stupidity, now there's a new way to get a rush."

Michael cleared some papers off a chair and practically fell into it. The papers included a packet of letters to his son, all marked "return to sender". With a grimace, he tossed them to the floor. He made a mental note to get up sometime and check his answering machine.

* * *

Two cops, Ed Warner and Bart Kaminsky were waiting by the coffee machine near the entrance of the police station. They were chosen for this particular activity for their size, moderate boiling point and their acquaintance with the person they were waiting for. Nearby a working class Latino family were talking to an officer at the reception desk.

Ed made a decision. "Michael's going to flip out."

Bart made a face. "He was born flipped out. Maybe we ought to meet him outside."

The two started for the door as it slammed open and Michael burst in. He was filled with despair and fury in equal measures. Bart tried dousing the fire with consolation. "I'm sorry Michael."

Michael brushed right past it. "Where's the accident report? I want to see the fucking report."

"Take it easy," Bart said, knowing he wouldn't.

It just fed Michael's fury. "Fuck you. Sara is murdered and all you can say is take it easy. Okay, okay, you want easy, I'll give you fucking easy."

Michael was suddenly quiet. He calmly put money in the coffee machine and watched the cup drop and begin to fill. "Is this easy enough?" Michael calmly picked up the cup of coffee and then violently hurled it against the opposite wall.

Ed and Bart eyed each other, acknowledging that this was as bad as they thought it would be. Ed got the nod as to who was next up. He put his hand consolingly on Michael's shoulder.

Michael was not going to be consoled. "Is this easy enough?" Michael said sarcastically as he gave Bart a shove.

"Is this easy enough?" Michael repeated as his rage escalated and he gave the cop another shove.

Bart grabbed for Michael attempting to corral him. Michael wrestled free and was about to slug him when Ed pinned him from behind. He shouted at Michael. "Fuckhead, it's no murder! The other driver is dead!"

Michael stopped struggling and the three untangled. The news sank in as they all caught their breath. Michael wasn't buying their story. "They blew it, that's all. They tried to run her off the road and bang."

Bart tried to explain. "There's no 'they', Michael. I've known the driver for years. There's his family over there. You want to talk to them?"

Michael looked over toward the reception desk. He saw a family obviously distraught talking to the officer at the desk. Overwhelmed, Michael sat down. "It was no accident," he muttered almost to himself, in confusion and pain.

* * *

Arens was on the road outside Trenton making a call to Everett. He had bad news. The person who made the death threat on the air didn't kill Sara.

"You found him?" Everett asked.

"Your NSA material helped. I guess he hadn't heard anonymity is a thing of the past. We had a chat." From Arens' tone it was obvious the chat wasn't casual.

Everett was disappointed. "We're going to be getting a lot of heat for this. Guilt by association."

"The irony is so far the person who killed Sara doesn't seem to be associated with anything."

"Even if he's a freelancer we've got to run this down quickly. I'm sure this has lit a fire under Michael Flaherty and he was already burning."

* * *

The marina on Long Island Sound was crowded with weekend boaters. Randy and Earl, trying hard not to look nervous and out of place, were searching for a boat along the dock.

Finally spotting it, they climbed aboard. Greeting them were Everett and six other men. Dressed like Sunday boaters, they were attempting to appear casual. Randy extended a handshake as the boat got underway.

"My name's-"

"Mobile," Everett interrupted. "Mobile and Montgomery, I'd like you to meet Memphis, KC, Indie, Billings, Phoenix, and at the helm, Austin."

The men exchanged greetings as Everett continued. "We all share the same beliefs and we're willing to die for them. That's all you need to know."

Austin took the boat out into the middle of the Sound. The men were enjoying themselves in the sun, drinking beer and having pointedly innocuous conversations about sports.

Everett was the picture of casual amiability as he spent the next few hours talking to every one of them. The talk may have been innocuous, but his sizing them up was not. Finally he moved over next to Randy. He seemed to set Randy at ease as he engaged him in some small talk.

"You think you're ready?" Everett asked, suddenly serious.

Randy took Everett's question in and nodded affirmatively. In the same instant, Everett grabbed Randy by the back of his head and jammed a commando knife against his throat. "Who are you?!"

Everyone was transfixed as they stared in disbelief at Everett. Randy was petrified. He struggled to say something, but couldn't.

"Who are you?" Everett asked again as probing as the knife in his hand. The group tensed, wondering if they had a traitor in their midst.

"Don't try to speak. Just listen. You hear what I'm saying. Every syllable of every word. Your eyes miss nothing. Your mind is racing, but your thoughts are focused and clear. Until now you might as well have been deaf, dumb and blind. You're about to die and this is the only time in your whole fucking life you're alive and not sleepwalking. You sleepwalk with your wife, you sleepwalk with your children, but I'll be goddamned if you'll sleepwalk with me."

The group was stunned. Everett released a badly shaken Randy. "You want an answer to who are you?"

Randy just managed a nod.

"Unfortunately, you're a helluva lot more than you'll ever know." Everett handed Randy the knife. "For luck."

Everett thought to himself he must be getting old, he'd given that demonstration a hundred times and it had never lost some of its edge before. It still enabled him to eliminate Randy. He definitely was what he said he was. If there was an informant among the group he'd find him.

"I want to call your attention to an interesting landmark on the right."

Everybody turned to look. Across the East River was a clear view of the UN building.

CHAPTER 16

Trying to be the sunset

Michael realized he was sitting again at the back of a group of people listening as someone spoke. This time he wasn't just being coy. There were two sets of mourners at Sara's funeral, those he didn't want to talk to and those who didn't want to talk to him. The first set consisted of Nime and the second of Jack and the others.

When Jack heard about the accident, he immediately thought of the caller's threat. He was devastated and furious. Hadn't he warned her. It would never have happened without Michael.

Even after he was told it really was an accident, it was hard for him to shake his anger. He was cold when Michael called with his condolences. When Michael asked about the children, he told him they were all going to stay with his parents and he had to go.

They were all sitting together listening to the priest delivering a eulogy to Sara. A liberation theologian, he was wiry and intense and obviously cared about Sara and her work.

"Words were so important to her. As the bible says, 'In the beginning was the word.' And what of the end? We are left with what was said, what was unsaid. Her words. Our words to her. Now made final. Not if we take it to heart. Then it will continue to live.

"We see as if through a glass darkly. But if our lives were bathed in light crystal clear, we would see no better. For the eye that refuses to see into our own lives is the same eye that is trying to see God's beauty. The heart closed to the suffering of others is the same one trying to open to God's joy. Sara understood this and strove to be open, caring and whole."

Michael came to honor her and to say good-bye. He knew right away neither were possible. He was stuck with his angry last words to her, "I'll see you around." He didn't want to be where he was. He didn't want to be listening to what he was hearing. It wasn't what was being said. They were good thoughts being offered up by a good priest. He still didn't want to hear them.

A different life and he might have been the one up there offering consolation and hope. It was painful and useless sitting here in agony. Not useless he reconsidered as he thought of Christ in pain and agony. He just couldn't do it, couldn't go through it to something greater. The only thing he could do was climb down off his personal cross and kill the people that did this to Sara. He couldn't even do that. He was stuck with it being an accident.

Nime kept an eye on him during the service, but afterward lost him in a crowd when Michael suddenly rushed off. Nime's intelligence effort was being rolled up. The only thing he was learning about Everett was that he was efficiently eliminating his assets.

First the woman in New Orleans disappeared. Nime tried to reach her contact, a jewelry store owner, only to be told he had been killed in an attempted robbery. And now Sara. Sara had left a message that she had something of the utmost importance. It was possible that she had told Michael. He had to find him. The State of Israel was at stake.

* * *

Michael spent the rest of the day considering his options. There were several. Yeah, get drunk or get drunk or get drunk one wise ass voice said. Sit down with your memories and your feelings and talk with her a wise voice said. Be haunted by phrases like "I'll see you around" and "It's madness". He would settle on one only to have the other two elbow it out of the way.

He drove around for hours. He drove by the station, he drove by every place they ever shared. By evening the family would be gone and he could go to Sara's.

He had no reason to go there. It was the blessed spot where he shot her kid's toy and killed their relationship. It was another destination and he didn't want to run out of them. The house was dark when Michael pulled up in front of it. He sat in the car and looked at it. More bad feeling. He thought about driving away, but got out of the car instead.

A wind had come up and was blowing hard at intervals. He walked around the house and surveyed the backyard. He half expected that the package would be gone, a phantom from a bad dream chased by morning's light. It was still there laying near the trees.

He looked lost and driven at the same time. The sound of the strong wind in the trees mingled with the whispered voices of conversation going on in his head. Bits of the eulogy and his argument with Sara and her family. "This is madness." "He's crazy." And then the cops sendoff. "There's no they, Michael."

He went back to his car and got his shotgun out of the trunk. He returned to the backyard.

The voices continued. They got no louder than a whisper, but began to overlap faster and faster like a stretto in a mad fugue, finally getting stuck on the phrase, "I'll see you around." As the phrase repeated, Michael played with the heft of the shotgun as if he were weighing his life. His finger tightened on the trigger. He quickly raised the gun and fired toward the trees.

The shotgun blast was followed by a sharp percussive explosion as the entire hillside lit up in a white phosphorescent glare. Tree fragments flew everywhere. Michael was knocked off his feet. He lay there as the reverberation of the explosion died away. He listened. No voices, just the sound of the wind.

He got up and walked out of the yard. A white Corvette with its lights off was slowly driving by the front of the house. As he appeared it suddenly peeled out and sped away. Michael jumped into his car and started after it. The Corvette accelerated like a rocket down a winding road. Michael raced to catch up. Rounding a bend, he spotted the Corvette.

"You like accidents. Let's have an accident."

Michael jammed the accelerator and hurtled toward the Corvette. He caught up with it on a curve. He focused intently on the spot on the car where he would ram it, running it off the road. In his mind's eye he saw the car smashed and the driver in it, but he never got there.

The Corvette hit a straightaway and pulled away. Michael pushed his car for all it was worth and his speedometer topped one hundred. He got no closer as the two cars came flying out of the winding road to the outskirts of Philadelphia.

The speeding Corvette swerved to avoid intersection traffic and went into a spin. Michael headed straight for it. A bus pulled out in front of him. He hit the brakes and skidded around it, and out of the way of oncoming traffic. Cars everywhere but no Corvette, until he caught a glimpse of it disappearing into a narrow side street.

Michael raced to the street. He knew it had no outlet. The Corvette was parked near the end of it with the driver's door open. Michael stopped, grabbed the shotgun from the seat next to him and cautiously approached. He aimed the shotgun, but the car was empty. So was the street in front of him. To the right was an alley between the buildings. He was standing at the only exit.

He peered into the dimly lit walkway. At first nothing but darkness. With the light behind him, Michael knew his silhouette was an inviting target. He quickly moved inside the alley, pressing himself against the wall. He waited as his eyes acclimated to the darkness. The blackness resolved into a murky view of stairwells, piled boxes, mattresses and pieces of scrap junk.

Shotgun poised, Michael moved along the wall. He listened, but there was only silence. It was suddenly interrupted by the noise of people cheering coming from a bar down the street. Then silence again. Michael waited for a sound, a sign of movement. He had no patience for it. "Why am I clowning around in the dark, this asshole killed Sara." Michael readied himself for a move that would draw fire.

A figure in the shadows behind a dumpster aimed an automatic pistol. Michael took a deep breath, and looked hopefully at his leg. In a half crouch he ran across the alley, winding up in an inset doorway. He winced in pain, bracing for gunfire.

"Dead or alive!" he yelled out. No response. Michael readied his shotgun. He poised to make a move.

"Try it!" a voice yelled back. It was a woman's voice.

Michael was stunned. "Who the fuck are you?"

"Who the fuck are you?" the woman sharply responded.

"What were you doing at Sara's?"

"Looking for Michael Flaherty."

Michael took it in for a moment. "I'm Michael Flaherty."

"Bullshit," the woman yelled back.

"What do you want me to do, show you my ID?"

"Yeah, I've got an army of assholes trying to kill me. You're probably one of them."

"And you're probably full of shit."

Stalemate. Michael tensed, thinking about taking her. Instead he shouted, "Suppose I am Michael Flaherty."

"I hope you've got some answers."

"About what?"

"Russell Everett."

Michael reacted like she had said the magic word. "There's a bar around the corner. If you're not there in five minutes, wherever you are, I'll be right behind you."

* * *

A crowd watched in Legget's sports bar as the Phillies were behind in the eighth. Michael sat at a booth away from the action. There was a distributor cap on the table in front of him. The crowd cheered as the Phillies scored. Michael couldn't care less as he checked his watch and surveyed the room. He impatiently toyed with the distributor cap. A waitress came up.

"What happened Michael, your car break down?"

"No, it's just a good luck charm. I thought it would bring me some company."

Michael checked his watch again.

"So much for good luck and charm," he said sarcastically. He got up quickly and headed for the exit. Tess suddenly appeared out of a crowd and Michael bumped into her as he passed.

"Hey dead or alive," Michael heard someone call out behind him. He turned and was startled to see Sara walk toward him. For a moment it seemed like a miracle and then a painful hallucination. She was dead and this was no time to be losing it, he thought as the woman neared him. Now he could see it was someone else who resembled her.

Tess took his look to be questioning. "I was checking you out with the bartender," she explained.

"So?"

"He said you were trouble."

"So?"

"I told him I already had trouble."

Tess walked to a booth and Michael followed her. Tess sat down, Michael didn't. He got right to it. "How do you know Russell Everett?"

"He's trying to kill me."

"What a coincidence. Get up!"

"What?"

"We're moving."

"Why?"

"Suddenly I'm a people person."

Michael forcefully grabbed Tess by the wrist and escorted her to a table in the middle of the room. "Give me your purse," he demanded when they had seated themselves.

"Who made you God?"

"You want answers?"

Reluctantly Tess handed over the purse. Michael started to go through it, first taking out her gun and pocketing it. He was surprised when he found a man's wallet. Tess responded.

"It's Everett's. I stole it. That's what I do, I'm a thief."

"Yeah and I stole the queen's tiara."

"Look jerk, my friend's been killed, and I've been up for three days, scared out of my mind trying to find you."

"Why me?" Michael asked, curious what lie he'd hear.

"You know Everett. I heard you talk about him on the radio."

"So you're a regular listener." Michael's response was laced with sarcasm. He began examining the wallet. There was a Virginia license issued to Russell Everett.

Tess raised her voice in anger. "I'm an insomniac, I don't sleep. You don't believe me, do you?"

"Not a fucking word. Big time war hero Colonel Russell Everett, you picked his pocket, just like that?"

Tess simply nodded. She waited quietly, she had a surprise.

Michael sorted through some receipts and credit cards. The credit cards were a dead end. Everett never used them. Sandwiched in between them was a matchbook cover. The Runway Cafe. It was hard to believe it still existed, it belonged so much to Michael's past.

He remembered the cafe and the small municipal airport it served. Perfect for short midnight flights that wound up in Central or South America. Everett arranged for pilots to use it to fly money and drugs in and out of the country. He preferred more remote airports like the one in Mina, Arkansas, but sometimes it suited his needs.

Michael turned over the matchbook cover. Scribbled in pencil was the note "Charleston 5/6". He looked up, trying to size up the woman in front of him. "You're a great thief...or a fucking liar. How do I know Everett hasn't sent you to set me up?"

Tess pulled a gun out of her coat and pointed it at Michael. Shocked, he immediately tensed. In the same moment he knew he had to somehow relax enough to let instinct take over to weigh the options. Is she a set up or insane person, dodge out of the way or grab for the gun? Her voice interrupted. "You know what this gun is?"

Michael relaxed a notch, she was talking not shooting. He replied slowly still sorting his options. "Smith and Wesson .38."

"It's your Smith and Wesson .38."

Michael started to reach under his jacket.

"Go ahead," Tess said.

Michael felt for his gun, but it was gone. Tess handed him his gun. Michael was clearly impressed.

* * *

The two emerged from the bar as it began to drizzle. Michael got into his car as Tess retrieved a bag out of hers. He watched her. It was painful and fascinating seeing Sara as a different person. A very erotic different person. He felt that sudden intrusion of fantasy into reality that signaled the start of his sprees.

It was clear that he was in that sort of place. He didn't feel strange that he was having a sexual reverie about a woman who almost killed him, and who might yet as his professional caution kept warning him.

The reverie didn't last long enough to make him wonder how an unbalanced guy could try such a balancing act. He was thinking about Everett and Shaw by the time Tess returned. Michael glanced at her car. "You better do something about the car. In this neighborhood somebody's going to steal it."

"Don't worry about it, I'll steal another one," Tess casually replied. Amused, Michael started the car and drove away from the bar. He got serious.

"Shaw is Congressman Allan Shaw from Texas. He's giving a speech in Charleston, and my guess Everett will be there. First I want you to have a look at some photos I've got, and then I'll find you a safe place to stay."

"I've got other plans. I'm going with you."

"I don't know you from anybody. You proved you're a great thief and you could have shot me in the bar and didn't, but maybe you don't like shooting people in bars, I don't know."

"If it helps you any I'm not particular."

"You still could be anybody."

"Anybody could be anybody, don't you have any instincts?"

Michael had to laugh. "Lots of them. Some of them say crazy things like never mind knowing who you are or caring. Or maybe that's just me talking. Maybe my instincts are a hundred percent right and on a nice quiet peaceful day I could actually hear what bright thing they have to tell me. Only I don't remember such a day. And all I can hear is just go with this woman. In the meantime you could be working for Everett for all I know."

Tess frowned in disbelief. "You've got to be kidding."

Michael tested her. "How did you meet him?"

"Through an acquaintance that was looking for a good time. He thought Everett might join us in a threesome."

Michael wasn't sure he was buying this, but let it pass with another question. "What did you think?"

"He was military and not the least bit interested. I went through the motions pretending to give it a try."

"What about the other guy."

"Very nice dresser. Very nice attache case. Maybe something nice inside. My luck he was carrying about three hundred thousand dollars. It was obvious I'd stolen a problem. I was getting out of my car when I could see I was being followed. I knew right away I was going to end up dead, so I just dropped the case and ran."

"Did they get it?" Michael asked, feeling uncomfortably like an accountant with his running tabulation of lines of fact and fiction.

"Yeah, but they kept looking for me. There and everywhere since. I was afraid to go back to the apartment, so I called. Kit wasn't there."

"Who's Kit?"

"A guy I do jobs with."

"In the mob?"

"No."

Michael frowned in disbelief. "Sorry I asked."

Tess frowned back. "Kit's Japanese. He used to be involved over there, but they had a falling out. He killed one of the head honcho's sons in self defense."

"You trust him?"

"I do. You work with someone with everything on the line, you can pretty well judge."

"Pretty well hasn't worked that well for me," Michael replied with obvious pain.

"We had a contact number in case of an emergency. There was no message. I'm pretty sure he's dead. Meanwhile they got their precious case back and they're still trying to kill me."

"And you don't know why?"

"They're professional assholes, how should I know?"

"Maybe you could be holding out on everybody."

"You don't believe me."

The understatement of the year Michael thought. "Don't take it personally. I don't even get the people in my own head. Anything else in the attache case?"

"Just some papers," Tess said almost casually.

"What papers?"

"I don't know. Technical stuff."

Michael looked at her incredulously.

She didn't care for his look. "Hey I'm not in the paper business. I just glanced at them. That and a blank sheet of paper."

"Blank, perfectly blank?"

"Not a thing. What's with that? I don't think it's about to give birth to a laundry list."

"Could be something that would make those other documents seem like wrapping paper. What did your friend think?"

"We were busy looking at three hundred thousand dollars. I was going to show the papers to one of my contacts who's good on these sort of things, but I never got there."

Michael paused, dissatisfied. He tried another tack. "I'm curious, why did you steal Everett's wallet?"

"It's just a thing. Personal reason," Tess said vaguely.

"What reason?"

"Leave it at that."

Michael didn't feel like leaving it. "You're a mystery."

"So's everybody."

"I don't have to trust everybody," Michael said still probing.

Tess fended it off with a painful smile. "I'm not the one to worry about. I'm not a long term threat. The word is I picked the wrong people, that's it cold. Nobody wanted that kind of trouble. For old times they offered me something uncut and a respectable funeral. So go easy, I'm the least of your worries."

* * *

Michael's loft was located on a street lined with small manufacturing businesses and warehouses. Michael drove down the block approaching it. His description to Tess of his research didn't quite capture its scope. She questioned it.

"What makes you think the guy with Everett will be in one of your photos."

"I've got enough lowlifes up there, I guarantee you'll get another chance to meet him."

Upstairs, Michael's lowlifes were already meeting somebody. Arens was inspecting Michael's massive collage of political extremists, intelligence community and organized crime. He viewed the photographs with an almost condescending interest.

He rearranged the positions of some of the photographs. "Not bad, for an amateur," Arens commented to himself. He picked out another photograph. "Although he's not up on some of my best work."

Arens crumpled up the photograph and tossed it away. He stopped as he heard Michael's car in the street below.

Michael slowed down as he prepared to park across the street. Tess was suddenly uneasy. "Keep going."

"What?"

"Keep going. Just humor me, at least drive down the block."

Michael reluctantly drove on and stopped.

"What's going on?"

"I feel sick, like when something is going to screw up. Maybe somebody is up there?"

"Trust me. If there is I'll know."

"What about trusting me?"

"This is important," Michael said with growing frustration. "Maybe you can identify Everett's friend."

Tess' reply was filled with a desperate urgency. "Forget maybe. For sure they know you're here and they know I'm here. We should get the hell out."

"This is ridiculous," Michael said dismissively. He angrily turned the car around and drove back toward the loft.

"Stop the car!" Tess demanded in a fury. Michael ignored her. Tess repeated her demand. Michael continued on. Tess pulled a gun out of her coat and pointed it at him.

Michael jammed on the brakes and turned to her. "Look, I've got the place wired. I'll know if somebody is up there."

"And if he's got friends on the street we're into a shoot-out with some well armed flunkies. If I'm going to end up with my brains on the sidewalk, I want Everett to be in the crossfire. If there's somebody up there, you really think it'd be Everett?"

Michael didn't answer and Tess continued. It was at lower volume, but no less intense.

"Listen, Everett and every other asshole I've ever met think they can carve me up any time they damn well please just because they think they've got a monopoly on violence. Maybe they do. Part of me still wishes there was a place somewhere where I could hide. But I don't see it that way. You want him dead, we'll do it together. All I want from you is to point me in the right direction, and keep me alive until I get there."

"It's not that easy."

"Neither is the alternative. In fact I think you're just like me, you don't have an alternative. Otherwise you wouldn't be chasing someone with a gun in a dark alley. Whatever you're supposedly hanging on to, a mortgage, hope, justice, forget all that. You and I are going to drive down this highway, find Everett and kill him."

Tess' revenge wasn't exactly his, but the shared passion was intoxicating. He drank it in a moment and then u-turned the car and sped away from the loft.

He drove on, finding himself in a familiar place. He had been here before, but this was different. Tess had a kind of abandon that took him hundreds of miles of highway and week of hard drinking to achieve. She spoke to him like out of a dream.

"You've done this before. Right?" Michael's silence assented. "Many times. Right?"

Michael couldn't believe they were speaking the same language. "How do you know?"

"I picked it up right away when I got in the car with you. There's a certain feel to it. Going off into the sunset with some-one. That's romantic. This is more like trying to be the sunset."

"A bloody one," Michael responded, with the sober weight of experience behind it. "What makes you think I can do this?"

"I heard you on the radio. You know this guy and you don't quit."

"Don't kid yourself, I quit. The only activity I got for years was throwing caution to the wind. I've still got a bum knee and it's not like being on the street. I've got stuff that obviously worries Everett, but I couldn't hang him with it."

"So we'll shoot him," Tess said simply, half joking and half committing them to a terrible logic.

Michael smiled. "We've either got a lot in common or you're just a great actress."

"Does it matter as long as you get what you want?"

"My trouble is it's beginning not to."

"Well here's to new beginnings."

Tess leaned over and kissed Michael on the cheek.

CHAPTER 17

The art of the impossible

Allan Shaw was looking forward to the interview. He was having lunch at a Piccadilly cafeteria in Memphis waiting for her to arrive. In his late forties, his youthful good looks and charisma were compared to John Kennedy's, his populist politics with Huey Long.

Several people came up to shake his hand and wish him well as he was eating. He had his shirt sleeves rolled up and a very engaging smile, and seemed to genuinely enjoy both the socializing and the crawfish etouffee.

Susan Wingate drove into the Piccadilly parking lot. A liberal graduate of Smith in her early twenties, she didn't share her editor's enthusiasm for the Shaw project. The editor, Myron Amberton, was hired in the hopes of reviving the magazine's circulation and wasn't about to pass up any opportunity to do so.

They got on together. He was not exactly Robert Benchley to her Dorothy Parker, but had wit enough to endure her calling him Lord Myron. She was colossally ambitious. Her dream was to go to Prague and rummaging attics and flea markets discover Che Guevara's diary of his exile there. The Journal of the Prague Years, as she thought she'd call it, would make her a bundle.

By the time she reached the cafeteria, she had revised her opinion of Lord Myron's assignment. George Wallace or Malcolm X. Politicians in America who were sufficiently foolish to open their mouths and have truth pop out of them often got shot. She could be the last person to give Shaw an interview.

One of Shaw's well-wishers was leaving as she walked up. Myron had strongly suggested she leave her sarcasm at the office, but she couldn't resist. "Playing the man of the people, Congressman."

"Try the gumbo before you accuse me of that. And until I'm knighted it's just Allan." Shaw extended his hand. Susan had to smile as she shook it. Shaw motioned and she sat down. "You want something to eat or drink?"

"No thanks, I got something on the plane. My editor was surprised to get your call."

"I knew you couldn't get Eleanor Roosevelt, so I volunteered to take up the slack. Seriously, you've got a point of view that's not for sale and I've got a point of view that's not for sale, that's a start. Don't you get tired preaching to the converted?"

"Never. There's so few of us, it's like family."

Shaw smiled and then continued. "I wanted to try something different. They're always talking about politics as the art of the possible, finding areas of agreement. But when you look at really great leaders, it's more like the art of the impossible, the ability to unite opposites. The art of the possible is getting people to act in their common interests. The art of the impossible is getting people to act in ways that are beyond their interests."

"You're talking about charisma and what I've read is that you have gobs of that."

"I'm sure what you've read is that I'm outspoken and dangerous."

"Okay, that is what I've read," Susan admitted with a smile.

"Why is everybody so afraid of being outspoken? It's always labeled dangerous. Bobby Kennedy was dangerous. Barry Goldwater was dangerous. And as I remember, it turned out he wasn't the one that nearly led us into World War Three. People seem to prefer the silent types that sell out the country without a word."

Susan took out her notepad and a recorder. "Speaking of dangerous. You've certainly been very outspoken about the various militia groups."

"It's a matter of being driven to desperate acts because the Federal government doesn't represent them. It amounts to taxation without representation. That sort of thing has well known results in our history. But I think people have lost sight of a greater danger."

"Materialism," Susan added, making a confident guess.

"You have done your homework. I think the cold war distorted our perceptions. Communism was very up front ideologically, very aggressive. So you could see them coming.

By contrast multinational corporatism doesn't announce its ideological agenda. But it's as big a threat as Communism ever was."

Susan knew that Shaw was something of an ideological maverick, but this still surprised her. "I don't think you're going to make any friends in those corporate boardrooms with that message."

Shaw smiled, taking her surprise as compliment. It was a point of pride that he couldn't be politically pigeon-holed. He responded.

"As a matter of fact I already have friends on corporate boards. They're just too busy competing with each other to pay any attention to where the whole thing is leading us. I don't think the Supreme Court had any right to wave its magic wand and turn a corporation into a person."

"The Santa Clara decision."

"And now Citizens United. The people never had a choice, it was decided by a bunch of lawyers and the courts. The corporations simply bought their privileged status and legalized a form of idolatry. Beyond that, the domination of profit over our traditional system of values has been a disaster."

Susan was amazed at his choice of the word disaster. "You can't serve both God and Mammon. That sounds like free market heresy."

"The real heresy is that people aren't even aware they're making a choice any more."

"On the subject of religion, how do you respond to critics who say you don't believe in separation of church and state?"

"Church and state should be separate, there are many churches, but not God and state. When it comes to values there's never a vacuum. If one principle doesn't govern our government then another will, in this case profit. If profit comes first, then Government is for sale, our country is for sale, our morals are for sale."

"Speaking of morals you've had a lot to say about drugs. You compared it to oil, I assume because they're two of the most valuable commodities on earth."

"That's true. But they're also both lubricants. Without them the wheels of civilization would come to a grinding halt. Can you imagine Washington without Prozac?"

"Talk about the great depression," Susan said straight faced.

Shaw smiled at Susan's joke and went on. "You know one of the first things built when people started civilization, were granaries for making beer. The workers had to be compensated for the extreme inequality of the system. Civilization from the beginning has been unjust, unequal, and uncivil. And drugs were there to keep it that way."

"So what's changed? You're not planning on creating a just society?"

"Only time and the people's will can do that. But in the meantime how about a real war on drugs."

Susan made a face and Shaw responded. "Did I detect a note of skepticism."

"An entire symphony."

"No wonder. Only one thing worse than having to have a government, is having an impotent one. Credibility doesn't come from a bloated bureaucracy, but from doing what you say you're going to do. If you say as numerous Presidents have, that you're going to have a war on drugs or a war on terror, you better have just that, and proceed to win it."

"And how would you do that?"

"I will have something concrete to announce about that shortly."

"That sounds uncomfortably familiar," Susan said in a way that suggested she might as well have groaned.

"It does, I admit. Same words, but I think you'll see I mean them. It's simple. We've got the government in the hands of special interests. Corporations in the hands of foreign interests. An army in the hands of the interventionists. Schools and unions in the hands of bureaucrats. I just want to see them all back in the hands of the American people."

"Your rhetoric's certainly warmed and ready, when are you going to run?"

"Speaking of warmed and ready," Shaw changed the subject as one of his assistants walked up with a tray of dessert and set it on the table.

It brought a smile to Susan's face. "Is that great timing, or does he always appear when you have a tough question?"

"Always. He's waiting tray in hand wherever I go. I know you said you weren't hungry, but how can we share ideas and not food. It's a crime in the South."

"Let us season together. Wasn't that one of President Johnson's favorite expressions?"

Shaw smiled in admiration. "I knew I would like you."

CHAPTER 18

A thief or a saint

A thought had almost killed him. Kit could appreciate it afterward. "Tess has come back" wasn't even a thought, a lazy hypothesis, a hasty ill drawn sketch of reality. In the next instant he realized he was thinking when he should be using his senses. There was no sound of her keys. He had his gun out and was firing as the two men kicked open the front door. It gave him enough cover to get out a window.

He had escaped them, but he knew they would keep after him and soon the Yakuza would do the same. He wondered if Tess were still alive. Their contact number was useless. Much too dangerous until he had time to sort out what was compromised and what was not.

He had no illusions that he could avoid being caught. His only chance was to stay alive long enough to find out something he could bargain for his life. He decided to pass along the information about the papers to the Yakuza.

Kit gave the Yakuza their first break since the papers were stolen out from under them, and they sent three men to meet him. One of the men hated leaving Japan and hated meeting the man that killed his son. But he was ordered by his superiors to do both. He was told the killing was now regarded as self defense and officially over. It was a gesture of reconciliation. Kit was waiting for them at the Hotel Otani in Los Angeles.

There were official apologies and then they got down to business. He told them about the robbery. He lied about Tess' identity. A woman had set up the robbery and had told him they were about drugs. He thought she was killed and the papers taken.

They made a generous offer for his help in retrieving them. He accepted on condition that he actually delivered them. He was broke and could have used the money, but it was the proper way to handle it. Any information they could find out was infinitely more valuable. It was the only thing that would keep him alive.

* * *

It was four in the morning as Michael's car cruised down a nearly empty highway 95. The car's interior was littered with evidence of life on the road, empty coffee cups and fast food wrappers. Despite the hour he and Tess were both wide awake.

Michael's attention was more on Tess than the deserted highway as she was going through the box of CDs looking for something to play. She came across Nime's series of talks and responded to one of the titles.

"Gauguin, you know I've always been jealous of him."

"You wanted to be a painter?"

"No, he gets bored of Paris and sails to Tahiti. Me, I'd just like to be able to get bored with Paris." Tess read some of the quotes on the CD. "Questions, secrets, what is this about?"

"Finding some meaning in things like sprees and sexual fantasy. Rather than just a problem, the guy thinks it's an opportunity."

"And if your problem is fifty feet tall."

"More opportunity."

"He's definitely an optimist," Tess said with a laugh. She noticed Michael was studying her. "You keep staring at me as if you were looking for something. Maybe we could pull over and find it."

Michael was intrigued by her invitation, but answered simply. "It's just you look a lot like Sara."

Tess thought it over. "It must be strange. Two people that look so much alike and are so different. I liked her from what I heard on the radio. But she was straight as they come and I'm all twists and turns. Put us together and we'd make a very interesting person. Maybe too interesting for this world. But with your imagination you're probably already doing that."

"I don't have to. You're less different than you think."

"I don't see me at college or her on the streets at thirteen."

"I get that. But I still think you're similar."

"You're disappointing me," Tess replied with a frown. "I thought from your radio program you're good on people. I'm just a thief. I'm not knocking it, and I'm not talking about sticking a gun in someone's face. It's an art not a mugging. Kit picked up on it when we worked together. He said it was like I was doing, what do you call it, that martial art thing. He got a laugh out of it because I thought he said Hi Kiddo."

"Aikido. Someone suggested it for rehabbing my leg."

"Kit said it's all about watching, getting to know someone, anticipating their moves and making your play at the right time. He really thought I was a natural."

"How did you get into it?"

There was an awkward silence as Tess realized with some pain that no one had asked her that before. She answered with a casualness that belied that pain. "I was young, what can I say. I figured it was an easy way to get even and money at the same time. Later I realized I steal money, jewelry, that sort of thing. What's been stolen from me I can't steal back."

"Tough way to make a living."

"It's honest at least."

Michael made a face.

"It calls a spade a spade. Look, as far as I can see all we've got is ours because we took it from somebody."

Michael face registered disbelief as Tess continued on."We stole this country from the Indians, am I right. They write up a paper or pass a law that makes it legal. I'm just honest enough or stupid enough not to hide it. I say what it is. So they've got the law to cover them and I've just got my wits. You decide."

"So we're all thieves?"

"Or prostitutes."

"I should have guessed," Michael said sarcastically.

"Yeah, if you're not a thief you're a prostitute."

"I don't see myself as either."

"So what does that prove except you're blind. It's a great gig. They cut you down to size, and as an added bonus they get to sell you back everything they took from you in the first place. You know the score."

Tess took Michael's smile to be a yes and continued.

"You want to be smart you got to go to the right college. You want to be sexy you've got to have the right dress or tit job or car or attitude. It's their ballgame and you play it good or bad, it makes no difference, it's theirs and you've sold yourself off. Or you can be a thief."

"Or a Saint."

"Okay. But that's not exactly in the cards for most of us."

Michael seemed to go elsewhere for a moment and then laughed.

"What's so funny?" Tess asked.

"I was thinking about an old adviser I had. He once told me to find God I should have an open heart and an open mind. Meanwhile I'm looking at your body and it's obvious all I can manage is an open fly."

"One out of three, not a bad percentage. Look. This guy on the CD is an optimist. I don't know about you, but I'm not. The only thing I'm hoping to find is Everett. We've got a fantasy going both of us like. We're both willing to play it out. Let's leave it at that."

CHAPTER 19

It's not easy undoing every wrong twist and turn
since Lawrence of Arabia walked into Damascus.

"Stop Shaw, Stop Fascism" was how their signs read. A small group of protesters paraded in front of a hotel in Charleston, South Carolina as their leader was yelling the same message into a bullhorn. Shaw supporters were carrying "Save America" signs, while police kept the two groups apart. Several news trucks were parked in front of the hotel.

Inside the hotel ballroom Allan Shaw was at a rostrum giving a rousing speech to a packed house. Behind Shaw were the South Carolina state flag and the American flag which was flying upside down.

"So now they're calling me a fascist. In the months to come you'll hear them call me everything, except wrong."

The crowd laughed.

"Their favorite is controversial. Anybody who dares to talk about who really runs this country, they call controversial. I even hear it from my fellow Congressmen. Allan Shaw, the only real independent in all of Congress, Allan Shaw, the man who flies the American flag upside down to make a point, he's controversial."

The crowd groaned.

"But I never hear a solitary word from any of them about the fact that our whole country is upside down."

Michael was at the back of the hall, surveying the room.

"Corrupt, hardly working people at the top, hard working people at the bottom. That's... upside down."

The crowd roared as a contingent of Shaw's security moved through it.

"Criminals can walk your streets, but you can't. That's..."

At Shaw's prompting the crowd joined in.

"Upside down!"

Michael moved nervously among the crowd, but saw no sign of Everett.

"Middle class families have lost their homes, their farms, their land, while foreigners own a third of America. That's..."

"Upside down!"

Shaw was working the room.

"When you need help, they talk about less government. Meanwhile they bail out the Banks with billions stolen from your paychecks. They take care of their own and ignore you. That's..."

"Upside down!"

"And where are our leaders? Busy stuffing their pockets with money from special interests. America is politically, economically, morally, and spiritually upside down. And you and I are going to turn it right side up!"

The crowd was on its feet in frenzied response as Michael left the hall, pushing past two security agents. He came out of the hotel and hurriedly walked around the corner where he met Tess waiting at a magazine stand.

He knew she was going to disguise herself, but he was still astonished at its effect. A wig, makeup and change of outfit seemed to make her a different person. It was obvious to Tess that Michael didn't have great news.

"Let me guess. Everett still hasn't shown. Five hours we've been following this jerk. Is it always like this?"

"Always," Michael said as if it was written in stone.

"Who the hell is this Shaw anyway?"

"A right wing Congressman. He wants to take America away from the foreigners, bankers, big corporations and special interests and give it back to the people."

"Sounds pretty good."

"Yeah, unfortunately it'll turn out to be his people."

* * *

The President had called a meeting to discuss the upcoming election. Clement Pierce would never be accused of having delusions of grandeur. He believed in limits. Not just term limits, but limits period. He was a self proclaimed poll taker, current watcher. Nothing wrong in that, just the opposite, to keep ego in check is a strength, to ignore reality is a failing.

He hadn't started out as a politician. He was an engineer like Herbert Hoover and he treated everything as a structure, government, political parties, even as fluid a thing as history.

You could get a little fancy in building them, but you were subject to the laws governing force and materials. You could be self indulgent and throw something together and watch it collapse after a short time. Or you could design and plan and build it to last.

Asked to evaluate his presidency, he'd say he preferred to wait for the judgment of history. That would be all right his critics said except history has gone to sleep waiting for him. Wags with a historical bent said his height was between that of Harry Truman and Abraham Lincoln, but his stature was between Calvin Coolidge and Millord Fillmore.

Pierce had read history too. You lose connection with your backing and you're out there by yourself. And the people that did that were either unaware like Hoffa or Johnson, or they had a martyr complex and wanted to walk off the end of the world like King or Nixon. But they were finished. The art of the possible, that's what politics shared with engineering.

He listened as three of his aides discussed the upcoming election. Two hours of statistics covering contributors, economic forecasts, demographics for both Pierce and his possible opponents.

It wasn't that any of this was news to Pierce, but somewhere in the familiar litany he might be able to recognize a new pattern. An aide spelled it out.

"All the indicators in the model we've been using still show you're well positioned for the election. Unless the interest rate goes up two points or there's land war in Asia. I take it back." The aide paused to deliver his punchline. A stand up couldn't have done it better. "If the interest rate is steady, you can have your war in Asia."

Everybody laughed.

"That of course is based on the assumption of an eventual two person race," Pierce pointed out.

"It holds for the most likely outcomes even if Shaw enters."

The President didn't look satisfied with most likely.

"What do we have on him and his wife?"

"So far she's clean unless we can get her on her spending habits. She travels to Europe on buying sprees. What Imelda Marcos was to shoes, Laura Shaw is to hats. She's charming and good-looking and tends to leave politics to her husband. She's as hedonistic as he's spartan."

The President wasn't impressed.

"Great, we've got Marcus Aurelius married to Marie Antoinette. That's some trick. Any trouble they're having getting it to work?"

The aide shook his head. "She came to this country to go to college. They met and fell in love and haven't stopped since."

"You don't suppose you could get Hilliard to at least dig up where she said 'Let them eat cake'."

Pierce's aides smiled. They appreciated his occasional forays into humor. He worked at it and it made meetings more bearable and elections more winnable. The mood lifted as they all responded.

"Hilliard's busy working on the money backing Shaw."

"If he's not busy working on his next mood."

"His bio should open with he was born in a funk."

Everybody laughed. Pierce cut it short. "He's a good man, just make him a little busier. I want to nail down this Mafia connection? If Shaw's going to make a serious run he needs serious money. And this militia thing. He can't have it both ways. Let's get something on him. He's been in the mud for twenty years, he's got to have dirt under those fingernails."

* * *

Cassis, a French restaurant outside Charleston, was started by two gentlemen from Marseille. They had liquidity, but didn't know Careme from cream sauce. A young inspired chef took it over. He didn't care for the decor, a ridiculous pastiche of French styles, but his patrons loved it so he left it alone and concentrated on turning it into a four star.

The mixture of Provencal and Normandine exterior was punctuated with trellised ivy. The Parisian interior came with a Muzak version of Edith Piaf songs. The restaurant was filled with diners.

Allan Shaw was sipping after dinner drinks with Hollings and political backers. He tried to ignore his differences with the people across from him as he patiently listened to their banter. They were gossiping about his run in with a reporter when he filled in the details.

"I told him I hate political labels, they're meaningless. But the reporter kept on, so I told him I'm an ecologist. I'm out to save the most endangered species on earth, the individual."

That brought nods of assent and replies. "Speaking of individuals. What about that Supreme Court decision?"

"That will put a nail in the coffin of family farms. It's a complete travesty."

"Happening more all the time."

Shaw spoke up. "The rich can buy their justice like their politicians. If it was up to them we'd all be living in the United Estates of America."

"Not for long," Hollings responded buoyantly.

He raised his glass in toast.

"To Allan Shaw, the next President of the United States."

As the Group raised their glasses in toast, Michael entered the restaurant. Pretending to study a menu, he studied the room instead. Shaw and his group were seated at a large table near the back. Familiar faces, but he was disappointed there was no sign of Everett.

Tess was parked around the corner. She watched Michael emerge from the restaurant and walk toward her. He passed by a homeless woman who was selling roses. He didn't seem to pay much attention, but after a few steps he suddenly turned and went back to her. He bought her entire basket of roses.

He dodged traffic crossing the street and walked up to the car. He got in holding the roses. For a moment Tess' face reflected a flicker of joyful innocence as she thought they were for her. She knew better. "I never guessed you're the romantic type," Tess said sarcastically.

Michael bypassed her sarcasm. "Ever sold flowers?"

"What? Oh sure, at the county fair when I was three."

"You're going to plant a bug at their table."

"Why are we fucking with this?" Tess said in disbelief.

"You're going to have to trust me."

"I thought you didn't believe in trust?"

"I don't."

"Neither do I," Tess replied in a tone that demanded some explanation.

Michael was impatient and not in the mood for giving one. He reluctantly gave one. "Everett ruined my life. I spent years in rehab. Every step reminded me how he was going to pay. If it was as easy as blowing his head off, I would have done that long ago."

With the help of a screwdriver, Michael wired a tiny listening device to one of the bunches of roses. Tess finished hearing Michael's instructions and then entered the restaurant with the basket of flowers. His instructions hadn't included carrying her gun concealed in the roses. She had deftly improved the arrangement as she left the car.

Tess began circulating among the tables, pretending to interest the diners in her flowers. She glanced toward the rear of the restaurant, looking for the group of people Michael had described. She was shocked when she caught sight of Hollings. It unnerved her. The thought that her gun was nestled among the roses was reassuring.

As Tess started making her way toward Hollings' table, Michael was sitting in the car. He was trying to eavesdrop on the melange of polite dinner conversation and faint French musical numbers broadcast through the bug. He was hoping Everett might show up for dinner and he could be the uninvited guest from across the street.

He heard dozens of voices, tinkling glasses and clattering silverware and talk about roses. He listened impatiently. It was getting late. And then amongst some other conversation he heard Shaw's voice in the background.

Tess was two tables away from Shaw's. She was getting ready to approach them, when she noticed the maitre d' coming in her direction. She was relieved to see that his attention was focused on Shaw.

Shaw whispered something to the maitre d' who nodded before walking toward the kitchen. Tess was wondering whether it was something more serious than a late dessert course, when a man dining with two women, called her over to buy flowers.

As she reluctantly carried out the transaction, she managed to see Shaw get up. Tess hurriedly finished, almost forgetting the money. She watched as Shaw disappeared into the kitchen. Tess whispered the news into the flowers.

Michael got out of the car and jogged around the side of the restaurant to the rear of the building. The back entrance to the kitchen had several fluorescent lights above it which left the nearly filled parking lot in shadow. Michael hid himself between rows of cars and waited. Two chefs and their entire staff were standing some distance away taking a break.

A Mercedes sped into the back of the lot. Accompanied by a bodyguard Everett got out of the car. Michael pulled out his gun. As Everett and his bodyguard approached the kitchen, they emerged from the shadows into the glare of the fluorescent lights.

Michael watched as the abstract image of his hatred came into focus as a perfect target. Michael found himself savoring the notion. He could see the bullet's point of entry, the muscle and bone torn apart as his life had been.

His hand tightened reflexively on the trigger. He was surprised how tightly, after all he was in control, not his rage. He was holding to that order of command. But why be difficult? This would be so easy and it would be over. He watched intently as Everett disappeared into the back of the restaurant.

He had been miles away from shooting him, he thought to himself. The tremor in his gun hand told him otherwise.

Tess had positioned herself so she had a direct line to the kitchen. She had already decided that if Shaw didn't come out in a minute she was going in. Wait any longer, and if he went out the back he'd be gone. If he's in the kitchen sampling Vichyssoise, she'll just give her apologies. And if Everett's there she'll kill him.

Michael ran along the side of the restaurant, looking for some kind of access. There wasn't any, only an ivy covered trellis that went clear to the roof. Michael climbed it. Straining, he muscled himself on to the roof.

He made his way toward the rear of the building. He stopped. A few feet in front of him the roof abruptly changed from concrete to glass. The dining room was visible twenty feet below.

The glass which was supported by steel struts spanned the building. There was no way around. He would have to go back and lose time, or cross it. He considered the risk. Forty feet ahead the roof was again concrete. The diners were in light, Michael was in darkness. He lowered himself gently on to the glass.

Shaw sat beside a marble pastry island that occupied a corner of the kitchen. Everett started to move a chair next to him. "I'm sorry I wasn't there to hear your speech in person. Excellent, especially the part about corrupt elites." Everett sat down. "I assume of course that you'll be different."

"Definitely. I hold myself and all the people with me to the highest standards."

"Good. If it ever turned out differently, I'd also hold you accountable. By your neck I'm afraid."

Shaw considered it a moment and then laughed. Everett joined him and they got down to business. Shaw reached into his coat's inside pocket and pulled out the blank page that was in Holling's attache case.

He spread it out on the marble topped table in front of them. He gazed at the blank page and waited for Everett to unravel the mystery.

"You want to know what we are baking," Everett said, enjoying the suspense he created.

Shaw thought of following Everett's culinary image with an appropriate quip, but instead proceeded to the center of his concern.

"I'm about to make two promises to the American people and I want to be sure I can keep them. The other papers have assured me about one. I assume this blank page has something to do with the other."

Everett nodded. "An update on the age old secret writing. I could have gotten the document to you in a variety of secure ways, but I can't resist a little stage magic." Everett paused for dramatic effect. "I give you The Salzburg Solution."

Everett began tracing his index finger across the blank page. A document appeared beneath it.

The piece of steganographic "magic" had its desired effect on an amazed Shaw. Everett turned to him. "It's absolutely secure. The only thing the paper responds to is my particular body chemistry."

Shaw picked up the document. "Hopefully this will be the solution, why Salzburg, if I may ask?"

"It's where the key meetings took place. Besides I plan to retire there."

The document consisted of tightly spaced text with some handwritten revisions and three signatures at the bottom. Shaw finished going over it.

Everett read Shaw's face and could see that he was clearly pleased. Everett proudly commented. "It's a start. It's not easy undoing every wrong twist and turn since Lawrence of Arabia walked into Damascus."

Shaw read over the page. "I definitely like the looks of this."

"The Israelis won't," Everett answered sharply.

"Don't worry. The Americans will when they discover there's no more terrorism and they go to fill up their gas tanks and they're back in the 1950's and the economy is soaring."

Everett took the document from Shaw. "This belongs in your head." Everett lit a match to the page.

Michael tightrope walked his way along the steel beams supporting the glass roof.

Tess knew her minute was almost up. She had her hand on the gun in her basket. She tensed it, preparing herself. She was used to tight situations, but this was killing.

She tried to stay focused as a rush of sensations started to fill her mind. Distant faces, the color of the kitchen door, a slight chill, the feel of the gun, the Edith Piaf song, "Non, Je Ne Regrette Rien", playing on the Muzak. Of all things. It was her favorite. Wait till it ends. Longer than a minute, but maybe it would bring good luck.

The maitre d' spotted Tess across the room. Annoyed, he hurried toward her. He called to her, trying to be forceful and inconspicuous at the same time.

"Madame. Madame."

At a nearby table a four year old girl, bored with the adult table talk, glanced upward toward the ceiling. She saw Michael's darkened silhouette halfway across the roof. The girl excitedly tried to get the attention of her preoccupied mother.

Tess gave a last glance behind her. She saw the maitre d' coming toward her and the child behind him looking up toward the ceiling. Tess' eyes followed her's to a view of Michael on the glass roof.

For a moment reality had a definite crack in it, opening a view of an utterly surreal world. Tess' stare mended it. It was definitely real and definitely a problem.

Tess looked at the kitchen door and then at Michael, trying to decide what to do.

The maitre d' seeing her look up began to turn his glance toward Michael. Tess walked toward the maitre d' trying to get his attention. "Monsieur, monsieur." Her attempt only partially diverted him. He started to look upward again.

Frantic to distract him she suddenly began singing along with the song on the Muzak. Her first tentative bars got the attention of people nearby including the maitre d'. He wasn't pleased and was about to interrupt her.

Tess gathered her courage and started singing in earnest. Everybody in the restaurant watched in amazement as the song built into a passionate performance.

Tess finished and the diners applauded. She glanced up. Michael was gone. He was hurrying along the concrete part of the roof toward the vents to the kitchen.

In the parking lot Everett's bodyguard scanned the rooftop with a night-scoped automatic. Michael caught sight of the bodyguard and dropped into a crouch and continued on.

He reached a large vent directly above the kitchen. He took a compact listening device from his coat and placed it on the roof. Despite a hum from the kitchen fans, Shaw's voice came through in Michael's earphones.

"An attack? What kind of an attack?"

Everett, who was pacing inside the kitchen, turned toward Shaw. "For all we know it could be government disinformation, or happy hour bullshit by a couple of weekend warriors. It's supposed to take place the night of the eighth."

"That's two days from now," Shaw said genuinely shaken. "I've heard rumors, but nothing like this."

Everett tried to calm him. "The militia might take a lot of heat. Don't worry. Just stick to your principles, leave dealing with the smoke and mirrors to me." Everett got up to leave. "I'm sure it's nothing, but I thought you might appreciate advance notice."

"With our limited resources I appreciate all the help I can get."

"Some day maybe you'll have your resources," Everett answered with an expression that intimated there wouldn't be a maybe.

Shaw ignored the intimation. "Let's leave some days to the politicians." Everett smiled. He exited the kitchen, and flanked by his bodyguard walked quickly to the Mercedes. Michael watched them from the roof.

Inside the restaurant the maitre d' was lecturing Tess. She was half listening, keeping an eye on the kitchen door. Hollings walked in her direction.

"It is an outrage," the maitre d' energetically exclaimed.

Tess tried an apology. "I'm sorry, it just came over me."

The maitre d' shook his head. "No, I mean you have the feeling, the passion. Why don't you study, train the voice, no?"

"I'm too busy," Tess replied, still watching the kitchen.

"Too busy for your own gifts. C'est dommage. Same for me. Is silly or tragic, I don't know."

Hollings, lit by several cognacs, stepped up. "Sorry for the interruption." Hollings smiled at Tess as he tried to place her. Tess readied her gun.

"Where are the rest rooms?" Hollings asked the maitre d'.

The maitre d' pointed. As Hollings walked away there was the sound of footsteps. Tess and the maitre d' looked up and saw Michael crossing the roof. Tess started for the door. She had a clear path until Hollings angrily grabbed her arm. "You were sexier as a redhead."

Tess saw the maitre d' coming toward her. She aimed her gun at Hollings.

"You going to shoot me?" Hollings challenged. He drunkenly offered his chest as a target.

"Kill him," a voice inside her said.

Hollings swore at her. "You dumb bitch, I'm on your side."

Tess slugged the butt end of the gun into the side of Hollings face, knocking him out cold. She dropped the roses on his prone body and ran for the exit.

Everett's Mercedes pulled out of the parking lot and drove off. Michael tumbled down the ivy trellis as Tess sprinted out of the restaurant. They dashed to the car and sped off. Catching her breath, Tess was still thinking about Hollings. "Someone recognized me. The sharp dresser next to Shaw was Everett's dear friend."

"Hollings?"

"It was Ted something or other to me."

Michael checked his rear view mirror. "Nobody's following."

"I cracked him pretty good. Did you see Everett?"

"He was twenty feet away."

"And you didn't shoot him. What are you waiting for?"

"I'll know when I get there."

Michael turned a fast left at the first corner. He eased up when he saw the Mercedes up ahead in traffic. Tess got her gun out of the flower basket. Michael saw it. "We're not going to get close enough. All you'll do is depreciate his car and get us shot at."

"Everett was close enough in the kitchen. I should have killed him. Obviously you've got bigger ideas."

"You and I are not going down as a couple of losers trying to off a big war hero."

The Mercedes went south on 95 and Michael followed it. He kept an eye on the taillights of the car up ahead as he concentrated on his listening device's recording of Everett and Shaw's conversation.

"So what are they up to?" Tess asked.

"It looks like some militia group is planning a wake up call for America the night of the 23rd."

"They're probably not going to be satisfied with hanging a lantern in the Old North Church."

Michael looked surprised. Tess didn't appreciate it. "There's no way I could know American history, right?"

"I knew you were bright, I just didn't know you were bright like that."

"Great, you and Hollings should get together sometime."

Michael's attention was back on the recording. "I'm trying to get a read on Everett's voice, trying to figure out why he would tell Shaw about some militia operation. Shaw won't distance himself from the militia and Everett knows that. He must have something -"

"Operation," Tess blurted out.

"What?"

"Operation was in the title of Hollings' papers."

"What else?" Michael asked impatiently.

"I don't know, I saw them for a moment."

"Try," Michael urged but with less intensity.

"What do you want, it was just grief to me."

Michael tried another approach. "Whose idea was it to steal the case?"

Tess didn't respond. Michael was still waiting for an answer when she said "Black...Forest!"

Michael stared at her in puzzlement.

Tess explained. "It just suddenly came to me. Operation Black Forest." Michael kept staring as Tess continued. "Something about trees in South America."

"What would that have to do with this? Are you sure?"

"That's all I know, you want it in writing?"

Frustrated, Michael knew they'd reached a dead end. "That was some piece of work back there. Thanks for covering me."

"It's just part of the job description."

"Well thanks anyway. Where did you learn to sing like that?"

"Juilliard."

"I was trying to give you a compliment."

Tess didn't quite know what to do with Michael's sincerity. A painful part of her seemed to grow and engulf her. Tess tried to ignore it as she had before. It was a familiar pain, but it kept pressing on her. She began self consciously.

"When I was a kid I pretended I was a French princess. I got the Piaf CDs because I figured if you were a French princess you ought to speak French. I guess the songs stayed with me. Like the one in the restaurant."

The innocent images were more fragile than either of them could linger with. Michael eased them out of it with a question.

"So what's the song about?"

"This woman who's been through all of this heartbreak, but still says 'I regret nothing'. Can you imagine?"

"You're talking to a man who's lucky his bitterness doesn't eat through a major organ. I remember when I wanted to be like one of the saints with his hands outstretched embracing everything, and keep on even when they drive nails straight through them. I regret everything."

"So do I, that's why I love the song. Crazy, huh?"

"Not really. Not really at all."

CHAPTER 20

Let's play Joan of Arc. You can be Joan.

No one in his party had seen Hollings get hit by Tess, so he joked away his having been out cold. "It happens every time I drink Madeira that's not at least a hundred years old." He had a terrible headache, but the night was young and it might improve. It did.

On the ride back to Charleston and their hotel, Shaw filled him in on his discussion with Everett. Hollings was hungry for any details about the attack on the 23rd. The FBI was all over him. The militia attack was something he could give them. It was no skin off anybody near and dear and it was patriotic for goodness sakes. It was a good feeling. The thought of making the call almost made his headache go away. Everett was counting on that call.

* * *

Kit took his time making sure he wasn't being followed before he went to see Sumiko. He had hoped it wouldn't just be time lost, that it might give him a chance to use other contacts to clarify his situation. They didn't, which left him needing her brother's computer expertise.

Sumiko and her brother Akira had been politically and socially anarchistic enough to be an embarrassment to her wealthy family in Osaka. Part of the embarrassment was Sumiko's casual affair with Kit. She and her brother were set adrift with plenty of money to go far away and stay.

When Kit came to the United States several years later he looked her up. She lived in a high-rise overlooking the Charles river. She had gutted the condo and turned it into a painting studio. Her work required a kind of free associative hyped up state encouraged by liters of green tea and breathing exercises refined in the Himalayas.

Kit had a hunch she wouldn't be thrilled about his wanting her brother's help. Sumiko hated computers, that was her brother's domain. They had divided the creative world neatly and absolutely in the manner of Portugal and Spain in the age of discovery.

Kit should have known better. Sumiko could move from contradiction to contradiction without breaking stride. Thoughts were just so much fuel for her imagination to gain momentum and reach escape velocity.

"Computers, they're the nave of the future. The world of energy is tragic, not enough to go around, information is infinite. It will get more and more subtle until finally it'll work in the quantum sea of potential, like consciousness."

Kit smiled. "That doesn't sound like you. You used to say that machines were a curse, that machine like aliens implanted the idea of machines in mankind so that they'd invent them and machines would take over the world."

"I still believe that," Sumiko replied. She saw Kit's confused look. "You don't understand contradictions. They're wonderful. I love contradictions. You know how they say the horns of a dilemma. I did a series of paintings. Dilemma is a very Picasso like bull with glorious horns. You have to see them."

Kit made sure that between Sumiko's verbal cascades and their love making he had her pass along his questions to her brother. Kit wanted anything he could find on Black Forest.

* * *

Michael followed Everett's Mercedes at increasing distance as they got off the main highway and the roads narrowed and the traffic thinned. The marshy, wooded terrain got denser, the traffic and lights sparser until there was just the two cars engulfed in blackness, seemingly several thousand miles from civilization.

Michael and Tess intently watched the lights of the Mercedes far ahead. They felt the tension of being in a dark, strange, end of the world place. Michael remembered a similar place and recoiled from the memory.

"I've been here before."

"Don't get mystical on me, this is weird enough."

"A place just like this."

Michael was lost in thought as the car passed over a bridge and a swampy river. He remembered the Colombian highway was so empty the ambulance wasn't using its siren. Between the pain killers and the adrenaline, it was just like a ride in the country, nothing had happened. A minute later he was sitting up, swearing at the attendant to turn the fucking ambulance around so he could go after them. They shot him and his part-ner and they were getting away. He still couldn't remember if he pulled his gun on the attendant before he passed out.

In the distance the Mercedes' brake lights went on. Michael turned his headlights off and slowed down in the almost complete darkness. The Mercedes stopped alongside a heavily wooded area surrounded by an eight foot wire fence marked "Private Property, No Trespassing". A bodyguard unlocked the gate and the Mercedes passed through.

Michael drove slowly along the road with his lights off. A nearly full moon peeked in and out of the cloud cover giving him an intermittent glimpse of where he was going.

"The dealers were tipped because the CIA was letting a Colombian paramilitary run drugs for help fighting the rebels. I was set up because I wasn't going along with the program. Years later, I found out Everett was the liaison."

"So Everett got you shot?"

"Indirectly. We were a small price to help support our local dictator."

Michael pulled off the road and started to get out. "Let's go. It's not often you get a shot at justice."

Tess pointed toward the dense woods. "Does the shot at it include marching through that stuff?"

Michael nodded. Tess changed her clothes. She put on a pea coat and tennis shoes and took off her wig. Michael looked up at the sky. The moon had emerged from the clouds which were dispersing. He pocketed the night vision gear he had retrieved from the trunk.

They began making their way through the pines and underbrush. To their left through the trees they caught glimpses of the coastline and the sea. There was a fishing boat far offshore going North. The two reached a wire fence. Michael gave Tess a boost and followed her over.

They continued on until they were almost in a clearing before they noticed it. Michael instinctively pulled Tess back behind a tree.

Suddenly everything around them was brilliant light and shadows. They scrambled for more cover as the headlights of three dark green vans parked in the clearing illuminated the woods around them. Their view was obscured by trees, but there was only the night sounds of the woods and nobody seemed to be coming toward them.

Michael motioned Tess to follow. Finding a path concealed in shadow, they moved in for a closer look. A group of men were digging a large hole in front of the vans. Michael pulled out his camera and started taking photographs.

Back along the country road a Georgia State Patrol car pulled to a stop behind Michael's. The patrolman at the wheel picked up the CB. Sitting next to him was Martin Arens.

In the clearing four men, Randy, Earl, KC and Billings had uncovered a metal silo. They pulled off the heavy metal lid. The silo was nearly filled with large wooden crates. They began loading them into one of the vans.

"Wonder what we've got here?" KC mused as he and Earl hefted one of the crates.

Billings was nearby and offered a guess. "From what I hear an M2 machine gun."

KC grinned. "The perfect choice to level the playing field."

"And probably enough plastic to move the UN to Canada," Billings added.

Michael drew a bead on the four men. He took quick snapshots of them. He watched as they finished loading. Austin and Phoenix appeared and started loading another van. Everett was nowhere to be seen. Michael gestured to Tess to wait.

Tess watched as Michael disappeared into the woods. He circled behind the vans. Through the trees he saw the men continuing to load the van furthest from him. The back of the nearest van was not in their line of sight.

Michael dashed to the back of the van and slid under it. He began attaching a tracking device on the vehicle's frame. Before he could finish, the rear door opened and Memphis jumped out. Michael pulled his gun. He listened intently for any foot steps. There were none. Memphis was still three feet from him.

Michael anxiously waited. Did he see me? Was he signaling to the others?

Michael heard Memphis shout Austin's name. He heard no answer. Shoot him and run for it? He started moving. He heard Memphis' steps as he walked to the front of the van and got in.

The engine started up and Michael hurriedly attached the tracker. He slid out from under the van as it pulled away. He flattened himself against the earth trying to conceal himself in the low grass as he quickly searched for anyone looking in his direction. They were occupied, but not likely for long. He had to chance it and made a run for the woods.

The Georgia Patrol car was still parked behind Michael's. Arens was sitting in the driver's seat of Michael's car. He was satisfied, his work was done. He had searched the car and pocketed Michael's listening device with Everett and Shaw's conversation. For his amusement he began playing one of Nime's CDs.

He smiled when he heard his voice. Small world. He listened to Nime talk about sexual fantasy and shamanism for a few minutes before commenting satirically in a Georgia accent.

"Shaman this, shaman that. The only shaman I'm acquainted with is the one who marched through poor Dixie to the sea. General Shaman."

Tess heard someone in the darkness and readied to fire. Michael appeared. Before he could say anything, an intense light from one of the vans flooded the trees, sweeping toward them. Tess and Michael turned and sprinted into the woods. They heard the sound of men shouting behind them as they crashed through the underbrush and kept going.

They finally ran out of the range of the lights. Struggling to find their way in the semidarkness they reached the wire fence. Michael hurriedly gave Tess a boost as flashlights probed the dark woods nearby. As they started to climb over, Michael's injured leg snagged on a loose wire. Tess looked back at him dangling in pain.

"Keep going," Michael urged.

Tess started toward him. "Always where you're weakest," Michael swore to himself as he struggled with the wire impaled in his leg. Lights in the darkness found them and there was an abrupt fusillade of weapons fire. Michael instinctively flinched then redoubled his effort. He pulled the wire free and they scrambled over the fence.

They came running out of the woods and jumped into the car. Michael checked the rear-view mirror as he sped away. There was nothing but darkness behind them. They caught their breaths.

"That was close," Tess said still shaken.

Suddenly a voice came from the back seat.

"Not as close as this."

Michael and Tess turned in panic toward the back seat and saw Arens pointing a pistol at them. "Just when you thought you were out of the woods." Arens laughed at his own joke. Michael made a subtle move for the gun in his coat.

Arens was way ahead of him. "You don't want her on my resume. Pull over, we've got company."

Michael looked up ahead. There was a bridge which spanned the waterway a half a mile ahead. Michael thought about a quick maneuver, but a Patrol car sped over the bridge, forcing him off the road.

A Georgia State Patrolman got out. "Pounds" was his overdetermined nickname, as he was English, fat and violent.

Pound's hands were huge. One made the gun in it look like a toy. The other mangled Michael's shoulder as he yanked him out of the car.

Michael tried to hold on to what little self possession he had by joking feebly. "Take it easy , Tiny?"

Pounds slammed Michael against the car. "The name's 'Pounds', get it?" Pounds began frisking Michael. "Friends are having a picnic and I'm here to brush away the flies."

Pounds found Michael's gun and hurled it into the woods. Inside the car, Arens had his gun pressed to the back of Tess' head. From behind, he seductively ran his hand down her body "searching" for her gun.

"Skip the pervert stuff, asshole, it's in my coat."

"Getting there is half the fun."

Arens pulled the gun out of Tess' coat while Pounds shoved Michael into the driver's seat. Pounds got in the back and handed Arens Michael's camera and bugs. Pounds was impressed. "He's a walking emporium."

Arens gave Tess a knowing look. "It seems both of you are very well equipped."

Michael remembered he had left the screwdriver under the seat. He might be able to reach it. Then what? Two guns against a screwdriver. He tried reaching it without moving his body. Nothing doing.

Arens looked over the three others and shook his head. "What a quartet we make. There's Michael. Not enough heart to be a priest. Not enough brains to be an agent. Of course from what I hear of your escapades they're not the best part of your anatomy. And Tess. If there were a heaven above you would have stolen the key to it. Don't get me wrong, I think both of you are enchanting. Such pluck and high spirits. It's just the old story. You have what I want and I have what you want. And then there's my friend Pounds."

Arens repeated it enjoying its sound.

"His nickname has such a nice ring to it. Pounds is definitely a Hobbesian creation, nasty, British, and short. We get along rather splendidly despite the fact that he has no taste for metaphysics. And me?"

Arens pulled out a zippo lighter and began lighting it and relighting it.

"I feel like Diogenes with his little lantern searching the world for an honest man or in this case an honest woman. I love asking questions, don't you? Especially with a gun, it gives it the proper urgency and weight. So what brought you two together? Love, desperation, fate, mutual interests, good sex?"

Michael and Tess were silent.

"Don't like interviews? It's good practice for what's to come. After all what's the last judgment but the ultimate interview. Don't you find yourself asking yourselves those basic questions, who am I?, why am I here? Incidentally, why are you here?"

More silence.

Arens moved the flame toward Tess. "Let's play truth or consequences."

Tess turned to face Arens.

"Play with yourself, creep. Maybe your friend here will help you find it."

Arens aimed his gun at Tess' face and started to squeeze the trigger. "Don't," Michael yelled as he lunged toward Arens.

Pounds slugged him in the head with his gun. Michael slumped unconscious, bleeding profusely. Arens' gun was still pointed at Tess' face.

"So now it's up to you. Something enlightening would be appreciated."

"Go to hell."

Arens slowly squeezed the trigger. Tess braced for the percussion and the bullet. Instead a squirt of water ran down her face. Arens laughed.

"Fucking asshole," Tess screamed as she went after Arens. Pounds grabbed her right arm and twisted it to the breaking point.

Tess winced in pain as Arens admired his squirt gun. "I think you'll be glad I brought this along." Arens flicked the lighter and put the flame in the ends of Tess' hair. He let it burn for a moment and put it out with a squirt. He repeated the process, letting the fire go longer each time. Tess trembled in rage and terror. Arens played inquisitor.

"Questions and answers, fire and water, understand?"

Tess glared at him.

"Now let's play Joan of Arc. You can be Joan. First question. Elementary and yet profound. What are you doing here?"

"Amusing a pus bag with eyes."

"That's a bit unflattering, but it's a start. Maybe you didn't care for the existential overtones. So many things to talk about. I'd give your right arm to know who you work for for instance."

Arens put the flame in Tess' hair.

"Let's begin by talking about bellhops."

Tess was silent. Arens doused the fire with a squirt. "How can you play if you don't understand the rules? I think Wittgenstein said that. It's simple. If you answer, the fire stops. Get it."

Arens relit her hair.

"Where's Kit?"

He's alive Tess thought as the fire grew. She tried to hold out as long as she could. Finally she beat it out with her left sleeve. Pounds wrenched her arm. Tess screamed in agony. Arens patiently continued.

"Let's give Joan one more chance."

Arens lit up Tess' hair. As it spread, she stared at him with an intense hatred. Nobody was going to break her. Arens was disconcerted by her toughness and Tess responded to it. She taunted Pounds.

"Your friend is jealous, Tiny. You've got all the guns, but I've got all the balls."

"End of fucking story," Pounds yelled at Tess as he raised his gun, set to blow her head off. At the same moment, Michael pulled the screwdriver from under the seat, swung around and drove it into Pounds' eye as he fired. Blood sprayed everywhere as the deafening shot just missed Tess.

Bellowing like a wounded bull, Pounds went to fire again at Tess. Michael grabbed his huge arm, trying to wrestle the gun away. Tess ducked, but watched helplessly as the barrel of the gun swung toward her.

She screamed as she saw Pounds' hand close on the trigger. Another deafening shot. Tess felt a burning in her cheek. Shot and going to die went through her head. An instant later she was still watching the two men struggle, trying desperately to anticipate the path of the gun. Their efforts seemed to cancel each other out, giving the gun a frighteningly arbitrary will of its own as it kept shifting and moving, firing and firing.

Arens opened the car door to escape. A stray bullet hit him in the shoulder and he collapsed on to the road.

Pounds, weakening, finally emptied his gun. The click of the hammer ended Tess' absorption in the gun's dance. The burning in her cheek wasn't a gunshot, she was on fire. Tess screamed, trying in vain to beat out her burning hair. Michael held Pounds at bay and turned toward Tess. He saw her hair engulfed in flames, and up ahead the bridge and the river.

Michael pulled away from Pounds. He started the car and slammed the accelerator to the floor as Pounds came after him. Michael sped toward the bridge, while trying to ward off Pounds, who was wildly beating on him. Michael shouted to Tess. "Jump at the bridge!"

Tess frantically reached for the door handle as the car reached the bridge. A half a mile back, Arens, struggling to raise himself, pulled a detonator out of his coat.

Inside the car, Pounds overwhelmed Michael and grabbed for his throat. Michael lost control of the car. It hit the side of the bridge and catapulted over.

The airborne car began to revolve. Tess dove off, her hair flaming in the darkness. As the somersaulting car turned upside down, Michael tumbled out. The gas tank erupted. The car, with Pounds inside, was turned into a rotating fireball.

The fireball hit the water, vaporizing itself in steam and eddies. Pieces of the car floated on the river. Tess came to the surface, but she wasn't moving. Michael appeared, gasping for air. He looked around and saw Tess floating unconscious. Making his way through the debris, he swam over to her and hauled her to the riverbank.

She was still. Already gone. Michael covered her mouth with his and blew air into her lungs. She was so still. An idea that was merely a familiar shadow in childhood, "You can't bring her back," found a voice inside him. He frantically ignored it as he tried again and again.

"Tess! Tess!" The words came inadvertently and seemed to try to reach into a darkness.

Finally with a painful groan Tess began to breathe. Michael's relief was wedded with agony as all his childhood strategies of reaching his mother in that defying darkness came back to him. He fought being overcome and looked over at Tess.

She appeared to him new as if life had always held her hand and made her journey a sweet one. It was a moment of grace. Painful in its passing as he knew he saw her in a light he had never before seen and might never again.

Van lights flickered between the trees in the distance. Michael pulled himself together and struggled to his feet.

"They'll be here any minute," Michael urged Tess as he helped her up. She was still painfully catching her breath. Michael checked his leg. Nasty, but it would have to wait. They were wet, burnt, and bloodied as they set off into the woods.

Across the river, Everett and Arens were standing on the bridge surveying the debris. Arens was in a great deal of pain. Everett couldn't help but notice. "There's no use sitting here speculating, especially when you're in pain."

"He had a camera."

"I assume he wasn't taking pictures of the Georgia wildlife, so get someone to help with the dredging tomorrow. We wouldn't want anything interesting to get misplaced."

Arens nodded.

"You didn't find out what they knew?"

"Relating to the other's needs was an issue."

"Well one of my needs is to rule out a remote but nagging worry. She had the document in hand, not much time but just possibly a lot of Intelligence help."

CHAPTER 21

Hell, even George Washington will hear it.

Tess and Michael, whose bloody head was wrapped in a torn shirt, struggled through the woods, totally exhausted. They walked on, still shaken by their ordeal, silent with their own thoughts. Life threatened, life saved, a baptism of fire and water. They blunted its power to change everything. There was no time for its dangerous promise. There were more immediate dangers. Tess motioned for a halt. "I have to rest."

"Five minutes," Michael warned her as the two slumped to the ground, exhausted. He watched as the lights of three vans passed in the distance. "If they don't discover my tracking device we might have something."

Tess saw the van lights disappear from view. "They left some people behind, didn't they?"

"Definitely. They're not going to be happy until they personally escort us out of this world."

Tess laid back and closed her eyes, wondering if their nightmare would ever end. Suddenly she heard Michael's voice calling to her. Tess opened her eyes. Michael was standing over her, hand outstretched. Tess took his hand as he pulled her close to him. In almost a whisper she said "Thanks for the life-saving back there. Nobody's ever..."

Michael started to kiss Tess when they heard footsteps. Panicked, Tess looked up. Arens appeared from behind a tree pointing a gun. He smiled as he fired at Tess. Only instead of a bullet, a thin jet of flames streamed toward her as she screamed.

Tess' scream woke her and Michael. It was dawn and they realized they had passed out holding each other. Tess was still dealing with the nightmare as Michael tried to soothe her. "It's only a dream, they're gone."

As Michael helped her up, Tess glanced toward the debris strewn river. "There goes the evidence it wasn't all just a bad dream."

Michael didn't linger on it. "We have to keep after them."

"It's a long walk to the nearest town," Tess said wearily.

"And they'll have people watching it. We better arrange for some transportation to avoid them."

"I'll see what I can do," Tess offered. "And after that, any bright ideas?"

"We track Everett."

Michael tenderly brushed some soot off of Tess' face. "And get us a new look."

* * *

For some time the Medellin Cartel had set aside a new smuggling route waiting for a prize shipment. They decided to sacrifice their lucrative passage in the interests of honor. In a cove twenty miles up the Georgia coast from Michael and Tess, a fishing boat had offloaded six Colombians and several thousand pounds of contraband. Not cocaine, high explosives.

At the same time the three green vans continued North, their occupants unaware they were carrying nothing more dangerous than canned cling peaches. The Colombians busied themselves loading the explosives into a van identical to the three green vans. They had explicit instructions that their destination was to be West Virginia.

* * *

Hilliard was trying to set up his day so he could leave work early. He had already figured out what files he needed so he could work at home and arranged to be informed if anything came up. The more he tried to speed up meetings and phone calls the more they dragged. It was a certainty like death and taxes.

He had made a commitment to himself to reset his priorities and he knew from experience that some other time never came. Hilliard was rushing through a social call. "I've got the kids. The older one has got problems. She-"

An intercom buzzed.

"Let me call you later."

Hilliard switched lines. "Who? Oh yeah, I'll take it," Hilliard said clearly not pleased. The caller was on a cell across the street from a small town shopping center in Georgia. The center had somehow escaped the depredations of mini-mall conversion that had spread across the South. It was becoming a historical curiosity like Williamsburg, Virginia.

Michael glanced at the cell. Nothing from his tracking device, Everett had obviously discovered it. Michael was wearing new clothes and his head was neatly bandaged. He kept an eye on his surroundings as he talked to Hilliard.

Hilliard tried to make it short. "It's a bad time Michael."

"I'll try another decade."

"Lay off, I've given you plenty."

"You didn't do me any big favors. You probably wanted to smoke out some people and you used me to do it."

Hilliard tried an air of finality. "So it helped both of us."

Michael wasn't giving up. "So you still owe me."

A secretary started to enter Hilliard's office with an armful of files. He waved her off. He said to Michael plaintively and with exasperation, "I'm getting the impression you think this is a lifetime proposition."

"Why not, what happened to me was."

"We've been over this. I told you if I knew the way it was going to turn out-"

"You would have done it all differently. So you say."

Hilliard tried a simple equation. "All right, you didn't turn me in. Now I'm not turning you in, so we're even."

"Turn me in for what?"

"Killing a Georgia State Patrolman. We got it bright and early this morning."

Michael frowned. "Okay, so somebody doesn't like me."

Hilliard couldn't resist. "A lot of people don't like you."

Michael didn't dwell on it. "I have news about Everett with the militia."

"That's not news," Hilliard replied trying as hard as he could to rain on Michael's parade. The parade wasn't postponed.

"What do you need, his picture on a post office wall?"

"I don't need a damn thing. We've already got it covered ten times over. You're completely out of your depth, please stay out of this. If it makes you feel any better you can send me your evidence."

"I'll show you what river to dredge," Michael said angrily.

"The same river that officer was found."

"I need some files, NSA, the works, starting with the agent who was killed. If they don't connect with a militia attack and a whole lot more, then call me a liar."

"You're not a liar, Michael. You're a civilian."

Tess, driving a late model SUV, pulled up near Michael. Her hair had been cut short and she was wearing a new dress. She had called her contact number with Kit hoping he had left a message. He hadn't. Michael admired her as he got into the car. "Vive la difference." Tess smiled.

"How'd it go?" Michael asked.

"I picked the car out of a factory parking lot. Hopefully it won't be missed until closing time." Tess started the car and drove off.

"What about Kit?" Michael asked.

"There was no message. If he's alive, he's not saying so."

"He might be figuring that's the best way to stay that way."

"Check the glove box."

Michael pulled out two hand guns. "Nice work."

"Don't thank me. Thank American Express and the NRA. What did Hilliard say?"

"There's a warrant out for me. Tiny was a cop."

"Obviously there was no written exam."

"Everett's using connections, so it'd be nice to avoid the police."

"Did Hilliard believe you?"

"I'm not sure, but he's getting the files. We're meeting him."

"Do you trust him?"

Michael checked the heft of one of the guns.

"I do now."

* * *

The three vans separated and took different northerly routes. None of them on a major highway. KC, Memphis and Earl were driving together. "I never expected we'd dig up anything," Memphis said, "I thought we were going through a dry run."

"Something to keep us on our toes," Earl suggested.

KC glanced at the back of the van. "I can't wait to open those crates. I'll bet we got enough in just this van, they'll hear it all the way to Washington."

"Hell, even George Washington will hear it," Earl joked.

They all laughed. Earl loved getting a laugh, but he was getting impatient. He had expected them to take a direct route. Instead they were going through Columbia, South Carolina in what Earl figured was a wide arc through Charleston, West Virginia to New York.

Everett must have his reasons. It was more remote and that was an advantage. Maybe there was going to be an unscheduled stop somewhere. More men and supplies. He could get off by himself.

CHAPTER 22

The United Estates of America

Hilliard was irritated that he had to deal with Michael. He could ignore this meeting, but Michael wouldn't have asked for it if he didn't have something. Was it beyond what he already knew? Was it worth having to meet Michael in a park in the middle of the night?

He wrestled with the decision. He also wrestled with Michael's knowing about the attack. The number of people with such knowledge was accumulating. It put everybody's mind at ease including the White House, but not his.

It would have eaten at him more, were it not for the fact that he was reassured by others that they had a stopgap, they had a man on site. He passed along his report to the White House hoping his proceed with caution advice lit up like neon.

The White House read his report and duly noted his concerns, but put them down to Hilliard having lost his nerve. They had more than enough confirmation that the attack on the UN was scheduled for tomorrow night. Both political and tactical reasons demanded immediate action. What did he

want them to do, wait for absolute certainty? Well they had
certainty. They had a man on site.

* * *

Shaw had scheduled a major address for later in the day. It
was to take place at a baseball field in his home town of Galve-
ston, Texas. Caterers, technicians and advance men were
setting up an informal mix of a press conference and Texas
style barbecue. Shaw would have liked to focus all his attention
on it.

Everett's warning about a possible militia attack had
changed all that. The last thing he needed as he was about to
launch his campaign with a bombshell, was to be put on the
defensive about his "support" of the people behind some ill
conceived attack. It wouldn't be better for Pierce if it had been
cooked up in one of his strategy sessions.

What was even more frustrating for Shaw was that his
efforts to find out if such an operation was in the works were
yielding nothing. All that his sources were telling him was it
was either government propaganda or it was renegades out on
their own. How could he try to head off an attack that no one
knew anything about? He kept trying to contact Everett.

* * *

Tess and Michael were a thousand miles away driving highway 95 in North Carolina. It was a beautiful day. It served only
to mock their mood. They were in pain. Tess' scalp was burnt,
Michael had a concussion. The adrenaline rush of their recent

ordeal had worn off, leaving them to endure their injuries with coffee and aspirin.

Tess offered him something stronger. It was tempting, but Michael had a good idea where that road would lead. He decided that he would go on trying to think things over with the counterpoint of a pulsing headache.

It bothered him as it had bothered Hilliard that too many people knew about the attack. It wasn't like Everett to leave tracks all over the place. On the other hand for Hilliard to seem that positive, they must have somebody in Everett's camp. Tess interrupted his musings. "You feel any better?"

"Some. In fact if I sandwich my thoughts between the throbs in my head, it seems to work. I've had these before. It's the kind of headache where you'd swear you've been hit by a heavy metal object."

They both laughed. Tess had something on her mind. "I know you've explained about Hilliard. But I still don't get why you trust him?"

"I trust the situation. He thinks I've got something."

"Do you?"

"What they're going to use as a back door for their plan. The airport."

Tess remembered one."Everett's matchbook."

Michael nodded and then spelled it out. "I know that one really well. They used airports like this for their operations. It's not a stone's throw from the major cities, but it's close. I have a hunch they're going to revive an old favorite. I was planning to check it out before we meet Hilliard."

"Because of a matchbook?"

"Pretty much."

"You weren't kidding when you said it was a dim hunch. I'm not very impressed with what you've got, but if Hilliard shows I'll be very impressed with how you played it."

* * *

The Texas style barbecue had come up to speed. Guests were enjoying themselves listening to a band play patriotic favorites. Shaw and his wife Laura were shaking hands with well-wishers. It was a toss up who was more engaging.

Everyone who met Laura saw her fashion model looks, her upper class manner and her extraordinary intelligence on display. They had no idea that these qualities were all acquired with considerable effort on her part. These qualities could have been distancing, but people still came away thinking she was one of them because of her grace and charm.

Shaw stepped to the podium and the band stopped.

"Today I thought it appropriate to officially announce my candidacy for the President of the United States!"

The crowd cheered their approval.

"I'll be brief. I can compete with the other candidates, but not with Texas barbecue."

The crowd laughed.

"America has always had a representative form of government. Now unfortunately it represents only the rich and the powerful. Someone should inform the other candidates this country is not The United Estates of America."

A mixture of laughter and voices calling out "you" came from the crowd. With a smile Shaw graciously acknowledged their support and continued.

"Those people you elect every four years are already spoken for. I'm not spoken for, so I can do a few things they can't.

"The folks in Washington have had a war on terror and a war on drugs and they've been losing both of them. I guess they're too busy waging war on the American people."

From the crowd's enthusiastic response, it was clear Shaw hit a hot button. He continued.

"Now I haven't been busy butting into people's lives, so I've had time to come up with plans that will win both of those wars. For instance, I know you all want a drug free America."

The crowd cheered, but a little uncertainly, like they feared Shaw of all people was about to offer them pie in the sky.

"I'm certain you've heard this sort of promise before, but I'll let you in on a little secret. The shameful truth is it's really possible. We have the technology to do it and have had for some time. I know it sounds hard to believe, but what's hard to believe is that the other politicians have done nothing about it.

"I want to fill you in on a few of the details so you won't think this is the usual election year eyewash. I've learned scientists have genetically designed an organism that will kill cocaine plants and only cocaine plants. They went to a lot of effort to make sure that it was harmless to any other living thing.

"In the operation that I will launch, the organism will be spread across prime coca growing areas of Colombia, Bolivia, and Peru. It will completely eradicate the entire production in South America. Using the same principle we will go after all the opium plants.

"Operation Black Forest will be a three prong attack on drug growing areas of South America, the Middle East, and the Golden Triangle in Southeast Asia. With this research we can take the war on drugs out of the Middle Ages and make it winnable. It can be done. So why hasn't the government done it? I know they don't have to answer to me. Believe me they certainly do not."

The crowd laughed.

"But they have to answer to you, if you make them. I make this sacred promise to you. If I'm elected President, every last cocaine tree and opium poppy in the world will be dead. I don't just say no to drugs, I say good-bye forever. And the same goes for the scourge of terrorism. I have the plan and the will to end it forever."

The Guests were stunned.

"It's really very simple. If you want a President who's your President, vote for me. The government of the special interests, by the special interests, and for the special interests, is going to perish from the earth. Give me your support and we are going to take back America."

The crowd applauded wildly.

* * *

There was no applause at the White House. The President quickly called an emergency meeting. In addition to his regular staff he had his newly appointed scientific adviser and the Secretary of State. He was hoping they would provide him with enough ammunition to label Shaw's idea scientifically and politically irresponsible. Kevin Rodzinsky, the scientific adviser, was not very encouraging.

"With the caveat that my review of this is on short notice, it's conceivable you might be able to fray it a bit, but you're not going to poke a hole in it. On the contrary there seems to be decades of research behind it, the stuff from Beltsville fills a folder."

Pierce demanded the folder and Rodzinsky got on his cell.

Anderson Phillips, the Secretary of State was in a dark mood, reflecting on statecraft in an era of international inter-locking directorates. Although the public saw the usual hands at the wheel of the ship of state, they were as decorative as the figureheads on the bows of old sailing ships.

The ship of state had become a supertanker, a computer guided ghost ship controlled by distant unseen hands. He was just another exhibit in what amounted to a governmental theme park. He eased into the conversation.

"You could proceed along the line that it would upset the delicate political balance in the hemisphere. It will undermine the trust we've so carefully nurtured, that sort of thing."

The President's chief of staff, Steven Hart replied. "That's fine, but the downside is, if we push it too hard, you care more about those countries than your own people."

Phillips offered another thought. "What he's advocating amounts to outright invasion. That's a possible approach."

Pierce considered it. "It might be. But it's tricky. There's a lot of precedence for doing just that. Shaw could point to Reagan invading Panama with a good deal less reason."

Phillips continued going through the motions. "Maybe we can get the Joint Chiefs involved. They're not thrilled about this policing stuff."

It was immediately shot down by Hart. "Unfortunately I don't think we're going to get much soul searching for sending some helicopters with the clear goal of ridding the world of drugs."

The President was getting more jockeying for power than ideas. He rarely got frustrated, but he was now. "Some of it's got to be classified or secret. Now that we're finished playing musical chairs, maybe someone will find out how the hell he got a hold of this stuff. I know Shaw is supposed to self destruct, but make sure he's in everybody's sights. No more surprises."

Hilliard was silent. He was entertaining the thought that if Michael could help him tie Shaw to the militia, nobody would care what rabbit Shaw pulled out of his ten gallon hat.

* * *

After crossing from North Carolina into Virginia, Michael and Tess found a gas station off the main route where they stood some chance of being the only customers. Tess went into the convenience store to pay as Michael gassed the car.

Minutes went by. Michael was uneasy. They made these stops no longer than necessary and it was taking her too long. He started to pull the car around the side of the store when

Tess suddenly appeared.

She wasn't in a hurry, that was a good sign, but her expression didn't reassure him. She looked shocked. She got in the car and Michael drove off. Tess didn't say anything right away.

"What's up?" Michael said with concern.

"Black Forest. These women were talking, said it was on the radio."

Michael was transfixed as he listened to Tess continue.

"They didn't know much, they heard about it from somebody else. They said some politician made a speech about drugs and something called Black Forest. The guy working at the counter didn't know, he was busy listening to a game."

For the next half hour Michael kept switching channels, trying to get a replay of Shaw's speech. He never did. What he got instead was the talk of talk radio, and he listened with growing irritation as the information came out in dribs and drabs. "I guess I deserve this," he finally commented.

"Your show wasn't anything like this."

"You obviously missed some of my off nights. Of course given the state of my mind I think I did to."

Finally there was a replay of the speech. The two listened in disbelief as Shaw laid out the details of Black Forest and his commitment to its execution. Michael was the first to speak. "So much for Everett's secret."

"Terrific," Tess added with bitterness. "I almost get murdered to keep a secret for less than a week."

"With what's at stake he'd do it for an hour."

"What for? What am I going to do? A small time thief is

going to take a paper she knows shit about, walk right up to the President or the CIA and say look what I stole? Everett's a stiff if he thinks that."

Michael tested an idea. "Maybe you know the right people."

"Right," Tess responded sarcastically. "The kind of people that get your ex boyfriend into debt and when he splits want it from you. So I did a favor to even up. Someone tells me to steal an attache case with supposedly no problems attached, I do it, that's it. Be stupid like Everett, go make something of it."

"It's easy to see why your employer wanted the papers. Black Forest might really cut into their drug business. I wonder how they knew about the papers."

"They need lots of friends and they've got them. We on the right side here?"

"It's a good guess with Everett, even if he's doing good, it's for no good. And then there's the militia thing."

Michael fell silent. "What are you thinking?" Tess asked.

"They went a little hot and heavy with us last night considering Shaw's speech. We're missing something. Anything else in the attache case?"

"All I saw was the money and the blank sheet of paper."

Michael thought it over. "Must have been really something. They went after you for just knowing of its existence. Unless you're holding out on me." Tess glared at him.

He went back to basics."So what have we got that's not invisible. Everett supplying Shaw with grade A rocket fuel for his campaign lift off. And what are campaigns about, a lot of money and a little rhetoric. If it was money it could have been some numbered accounts in a cozy bank in Zurich. If it was something to back up his rhetoric-"

Tess remembered Shaw's speech. "The other papers were about his war on drugs. What about his war on terror?"

Michael pursued the thought. "A secret next generation drone to win that war. It's programmed to make its own tactical decisions."

Almost immediately it didn't sit right with Michael. "No, I've heard Shaw. America out of the Middle East, the Middle East out of America sort of thing."

"There's still his wallet," Tess suggested. "Maybe you're right about that matchbook. They're going to use that airport. But how could he think I would know about it?"

"Maybe he thought your partner did. Or maybe he thought you were professional enough to be more than a thief, maybe you had Intelligence connections."

Tess interrupted Michael's speculation. "I'll give you a better maybe. A big one. Maybe I should have just shot Everett in that kitchen and we wouldn't be talking about maybes."

* * *

It was Sumiko who told Kit about Shaw's speech. Kit was plowing his way through the database provided by her brother. The list of scientists who could be involved in Black Forest was endless. And there were more to come. Akira had asked him for some criteria they could use to narrow the search. How about nationality or age or area of specialization?

"How about recently murdered," Kit finally responded. If

the dealer was killed maybe the scientist shared his fate.

"Great filter," Akira replied.

Kit had a second thought. "They could have made it look like an accident."

"You'll still have a very short list," Akira concluded with a promise to get right back to him.

Kit knew he was reaching, but he still had a good feeling about it. That is until Sumiko interrupted him. Black Forest was now public. There were no dead Black Forest scientists to speculate about. There was no reason to wait around for Akira's reply. Kit went out for some air while he considered his own chances of mortality.

* * *

The van with KC, Memphis and Earl arrived in Charleston, West Virginia. Earl went to get a pack of cigarettes. He didn't come back. KC sent Memphis to go look for him. Memphis came back without Earl and they drove on.

CHAPTER 23

A very pregnant nothing

Hilliard was at home when he got the call. He asked to be notified if there was any change in status. The agent calling sounded annoyed. Hilliard knew exactly how he felt. He swore when he was an agent that he would never be a meddling, out of touch bureaucrat.

Bad news. Their on site contact was late reporting. Then came reassurance. "It's not of immediate concern, he'll find his spot. It's a lot of hours until tomorrow midnight. We've got them bracketed, those trucks aren't going anywhere without us being all over them. Not to mention what we already have waiting for them at the UN."

Hilliard got off the phone, definitely not reassured. He took a pill and began to live with the worst possibilities.

* * *

Everett and his team drove up into the hills of Eastern West Virginia where he was confident the FBI wouldn't be able to follow too closely. The FBI had heard from Earl that Everett planned to make a stop there, so they weren't surprised. It made it easier to maintain a moving perimeter surrounding Everett's convoy.

Everett had the vans parked at a remote property and when it got dark they buried them. The FBI's perimeter was on all the roads. One by one Everett's team made their way through the woods in between them.

* * *

It was seven thirty when Michael and Tess reached the municipal airport in Pennsylvania. They were meeting Hilliard at eleven in Washington and didn't have a lot of time. Michael hurriedly checked the Runway Cafe, pilots and planes.

While the look of the place hadn't changed much, there were all new names and faces. He didn't find anything. Michael and Tess started back toward Washington. "Still think they're going to use this place?" Tess asked expecting a "no".

She was surprised when Michael said "definitely".

"You must have seen something you're not telling me."

"Nothing."

"Nothing?"

"A very pregnant nothing," Michael said with emphasis.

Tess repeated "A pregnant nothing," savoring the phrase. "No wonder your friends at the DEA called you Young Ahab. You don't even need a white whale, an invisible one will do."

Michael smiled and then explained himself. "Nobody even heard of Everett. I take it to mean he's allowed this field to lie fallow long enough. I'm sure they're coming through here."

Tess weighed out both logic and instinct and agreed. "We'll camp out here tomorrow night. If you can convince Hilliard, we'll have company. Or we'll do it alone."

* * *

The FBI got a tip about a green van on the other side of the Shenandoahs near Harrisonburg and highway 81. They couldn't verify it. They got nervous, especially after they found a dirt access road through the woods past where their perimeter was. There was no sign of vans or anybody on the property. They checked all the roads, nothing.

Hilliard was passed the word that they were gone. No trucks, no team. No contact whatsoever. On site could still suddenly appear, the vans still could be sighted, things could go as planned in New York. It wasn't in Hilliard's nature to count on any of that.

The news gave his upcoming meeting with Michael a definite upgrade. Leave it to the chance of a one on one with someone as volatile as Michael? He could be a big hero if it worked, but if he screwed up it better be by the book.

* * *

Michael had known the park in Washington in better days. He remembered it being filled with families, teenagers, lovers, dog walkers and Frisbee throwers. Now the few who remained seemed totally out of place in the same tract of land occupied by the homeless, drunks and drug dealers. They were all in small tight clustered groups separated by lots of empty space.

This urban universe was not expanding, but its inhabitants were still drifting further and further apart. "Great meeting place," Tess said sarcastically as she and Michael drove around the park.

"It's changed. But I didn't choose it for the atmosphere. It's relatively empty."

"So are a lot of places at this hour."

"I once chased a dealer in this park, and he had a neat way of losing me. If we need to get lost tonight, we'll do what he did."

First setting up their escape route, Michael and Tess parked the car and sat on a bench overlooking the dimly lit park and waited for Hilliard. The park emptied except for those that got high in it or called it home. Tess checked her watch. It was eleven thirty. "He's always late," Michael explained.

"You know, one way of being very late is not showing up."

Ten minutes later Michael spotted a car pulling to a stop along the edge of the park. Hilliard got out and started toward them, carrying a file folder. Michael managed a smile as Hilliard waved the folder.

Michael's smile vanished as two unmarked cars came to a stop near Hilliard's. Hilliard turned to see what Michael was looking at and knew he had a definite problem. "They're not with me!"

"Fuck you," Michael yelled. He motioned to Tess. "Get the car." Tess disappeared into the trees behind them. Michael drew his gun.

Hilliard was flabbergasted. "You crazy motherfucker."

"A little louder so they can pick it up on your wire."

Hilliard shook his head in disbelief. "I don't have to take this shit." He tossed the file folder to the ground. "Now you've got what you wanted. I need what you've got fast. I just heard there's been some sort of firefight and agents killed."

Michael was stunned. He started toward the file, but suddenly froze. Two park "homeless" were ambling in his direction. Hilliard reached into his coat. Michael fired over Hilliard's shoulder sending him to the ground. Michael dashed through the trees behind him.

Tess was parked in an alleyway with the engine running. Michael jumped a nearby fence, got in the car and Tess sped off. Michael was hyperventilating with rage.

"He owed you one and he set you up?"

Michael didn't answer. Instead he turned the news on. Preliminary reports mentioned two FBI agents killed another wounded near Harrisonburg by unknown assailants.

Eye witnesses reported hearing automatic weapons fire and seeing a green van speeding away from the scene. Michael listened critically as one witness said the men looked like militia members. "It's too pat, he's been coached."

"How can you be so sure?" Tess asked.

Michael continued to concentrate on the broadcast as he answered. "When I was in the DEA I had to handle hundreds of informants and witnesses. You learn to tell the difference between bullshit and truth or you get hurt or die."

Michael thought it over for a moment and made a decision. "Let's get to that airport."

"You think they're already headed there. What about the attack?"

"There isn't going to be an attack. There never was. It's part of Everett's plan to make the government think this whole thing is a militia attack."

"He wants them to go after the militia."

"Precisely. Then the militia steps up their war, and we have chaos. Enter Allan Shaw. Everett has had plenty of practice destabilizing other governments, he thought he'd try ours."

"So he's not finished?"

"He's just beginning."

CHAPTER 24

A Puerto Rican salsa band

Tess saw the plane in the sky even before they reached the airport. She pointed it out to Michael. It was still gaining altitude, heading southwest. All they could do was hope it wasn't Everett's.

They continued on to the airport. It was deserted. Michael and Tess sat in the darkness and waited. They heard a news report that the FBI had found the green van, abandoned and filled with explosives. After forty five minutes Michael and Tess knew they had missed Everett.

They tried the local motels. Tess went in to check them out. It was a small town and the middle of the night. Everyone was asleep and hadn't heard the news. Tess described Everett and the others, pretending to be looking for a group of friends. The only group through recently besides the local Kiwanis was a Puerto Rican salsa band traveling from a concert in Pittsburgh to one in Philadelphia.

They drove to an all night convenience store. Tess bought a bag of ice and two coffees and returned to the car. As Michael wrapped his leg with the ice, Tess tried her contact number. She listened intently.

"Kit's definitely alive. He left a message. Sort of paranoid, like he thought someone might be listening. He said if I'm enjoying my vacation, he advised prolonging it. Otherwise I could meet him at three today."

"That's it?"

Tess nodded.

"What did he sound like besides paranoid?"

"Like he's got something going."

"Any clue?" Michael asked, then realized Tess would have said so even before she shook her head. "Where's the meeting?"

"Cambridge. He has a girlfriend there."

"Okay," Michael responded, but his mind was elsewhere. Cambridge. Sara had picked him up when one of his benders had ended up there. It was the beginning of their romance. He thought of Sara. Her message to him. The sound of her voice. She had something very important. What happened to it?

"First I want to try to find Sara's source of information while we still can. Hilliard's going to have the government after us and I'm already wanted for murder. There's only limited time before things get too tight to breathe."

* * *

Two hours later, the plane that had taken off as Michael and Tess got to the airport, crashed in a remote part of the Alleghenies. Everett had left explicit instructions as to when the news was to be made public.

CHAPTER 25

Mona Lisa couldn't do it better

There was an emergency meeting at the White House. Everybody expected Pierce to be unraveled. He could have raged about the breakdown of intelligence, or being made to look foolish.

Pierce didn't rage. Reason had to prevail in all situations or lose its province. If history did come calling, you had to be ready with a response.

Pierce's aides summarized the obvious one. Start drafting a speech calling for tougher legislation aimed at the militia. There were calls claiming militia responsibility as well as prompt denials and claims of a frame up by the government. Connect Shaw to any of this, and they can knock him out of the race before he's even started.

Hilliard was contacted and leaned on to fall in line. Did he have anything that would contradict militia involvement? It was too early he cautioned. He tried to make his warning emphatic, but in the back of his mind was a direct path from Michael to Everett to the militia. As he signed off he knew the

President would proceed unless he produced ample evidence to the contrary.

* * *

Hollings was more than surprised. He felt betrayed. He thought he had accomplished a number of things by tipping off the FBI. If it turned out to be nothing, he had a chance to play the patriot and get them off his back at the same time. If it turned out to be a real threat, the FBI would be positioned to stop it without bloodshed. Shaw would be saved considerable embarrassment and any election hopes.

Hollings had just arrived at a party when he heard the news. He sat in his car and listened to the reports. His worst fear was that Shaw would respond with one of his shoot from the hip remarks. Shaw's wife didn't make it any easier. Laura was outspoken when she should be silent and silent when she should be outspoken. Hollings rushed to Shaw's house to try to head off disaster.

He got there expecting to find Shaw and his wife following the TV reports word by word in a serious if not somber mood. Instead Laura was having fun trying on hats, while Shaw was chatting affably on the phone.

Their bizarre detachment did nothing to set Holling's mind at ease. He kept motioning for Shaw to get off the phone. He finally did.

Hollings smiled nervously. "I hope you're allowing your remarks to ripen a bit before you start shipping them out."

"I haven't given away the ranch," Shaw responded.

Laura noticed Hollings' critical look. "You don't like my hat?"

"No, the hat's okay, it's just this doesn't seem to be the time for such things."

"What better time. If we're going to do battle, let's do it in style. Or do you think being drab will improve our chances?"

Hollings was set to respond when he heard a commentator on the TV mention Shaw's name. "Here it comes," Holllings warned.

The commentator spelled it out. "If it turns out that the militia were involved, and this is pure speculation at this point, it would stop the momentum from Shaw's announcement speech. Pierce would do everything to tie Shaw to it and keep him tied to it. It would be a death sentence to Shaw's chances in the upcoming election."

Laura waved her hand dismissively. "It's just pay back time for Pierce's help with that legislation. They should force them to say this is a paid political announcement."

"This is just for openers," Hollings responded. "They'll have everybody including the Mormon Tabernacle Choir singing the same song before they're through."

The three fell silent.

"You think the militia were involved?" Shaw finally asked Hollings.

His answer came quickly. "The sooner you can go on the record denouncing them the better it will be."

"That's what President Pierce will do," Laura responded angrily, "Allan doesn't back down."

"This is no place for South American machismo," Hollings shot back. "It may be good for your sex life, but he's running for President not caudillo."

Hollings expected Laura's angry response, instead she smiled. Mona Lisa couldn't do it better Hollings thought and then apologized. "Forget the crack about your sex life, I'm just jealous. But if he loses support over this he gets dangerously weak."

"So Allan loses, at least it's not some shadow of himself."

"You're missing the point. Allan's already a target, he becomes a vulnerable one. I know what's good about him is that he's not so self protective he can stand for something, but what good is all that if he gets himself killed."

Hollings ended the sentence with as much emphasis as he could muster, but still wasn't getting through. He tried another tack. "Either you two know something I don't, or I've got to get hold of some of the air you breathe. You might be satisfied with a commemorative statue of Allan with an inscription about a dead hero who stood for what he believed in. I just hope I can convince everyone he'd never implement that Middle Eastern plan of his and this drug thing. Then maybe he'll live long enough to outgrow his current penchant for way over the top politics and develop into an effective leader and actually change this country for the better."

* * *

It was five in the morning and still dark when Michael and Tess got to Sara's. The security system was easy for Michael to disable. As he worked on it he wished it was more challenging. Instead of occupying him, it left too much room for the throbbing pain in his knee and replaying all the things he should have done to save Sara.

Having Tess there helped him to stay focused. What he didn't need was some absentminded mistake that brought out the patrol. "Let's just stick to fucking up the big things," he said to himself.

Michael gave a last survey of the street before letting Tess and himself in. They began searching the pitch dark house. Tess took the upstairs, Michael the down. Everything was neat, abandoned and lifeless. Michael sat at Sara's desk in her workroom. There was a touching photo of her and her family. He allowed himself a brief glance at it before turning his attention elsewhere. He was looking for answers not tears.

It was hard enough seeing her in all her articles and research, all the work and heart and hope brought to an end. He went through them all, including her most recent papers she had shown him at the radio station. The contents of her computer didn't appear promising. He made copies of all the files.

Tess joined him carrying a vintage beaded handbag of Sara's. They went through it together, emptying the contents on the desktop. It contained a set of house keys, a wallet, makeup and a cellphone.

Seeing them there, Michael felt uncomfortably like he was performing an autopsy. It was distasteful, almost sacrilegious, but he wanted more than anything to know the cause of death.

He expectantly went through the cell, there just might be something. Unfortunately it hadn't been used in months and he had to go through the pain of hearing one of his old voice mails to Sara. He downloaded the contents of the phone.

As they left the house, Michael knew they hadn't got what he was looking for. They headed out on 95 toward Boston.

CHAPTER 26

*This isn't Guatemala. I'll be damned if we'll be
destabilized by some ex CIA mercenary.*

The FBI was still in the initial stages of investigating the
contents of the shooter's van, but already there was a clear link
between the reports filed by the agent following Everett and the
killings. Everett disappeared with three green vans, one of
them appeared to be at the scene. The agent heard Everett's
vans were loaded with explosives, so was this one.

The media was getting leaks of all this information pointing to the involvement of the militia. The President didn't like
it. In addition to making it look like he was learning what was
going on from CNN, the public response meant Pierce had to
take some action.

The President had his speech writer prepare an address
asking for ramping up anti terrorist legislation. There was the
question of alluding to the militias. He put in a call to Hilliard
as his aides debated the content of the address. The consensus
was that they wanted to at least indirectly hit the militias and
Shaw. Without it the speech seemed vague and weak.

The President asked Hilliard once again if he had anything contradicting militia involvement. Hilliard was well aware everything pointed in that direction. He reluctantly told the President about Michael's lost evidence about the militia and Everett.

Hilliard knew that it would help ice the case for militia involvement and it made him very uneasy. The President cut short Hilliard's cautioning remarks.

"If finding this guy is so crucial, why the hell isn't the Bureau going public yet with his involvement?"

"There's a chance that the people involved in this don't know that Flaherty was right in the middle of it. The Bureau would like to keep it that way. It might mean we get to him first."

Two hours later Hilliard heard that Pierce was planning a major address prime time that evening. He called the President. He told Pierce that the agency was devoting considerable resources to finding Michael and to delay the speech until he was found.

In the end Pierce compromised. He decided to go ahead with the speech, but have it carefully revised line by line.

* * *

Kit was hoping that wouldn't show. Even if it meant giving up the pleasure of seeing the look on her face when he told her about the money. What she didn't need was more danger and that's what he had to offer. He wondered if she would choose to be free instead.

There was no way she would. The money involved was too good to pass up. A possible fortune.

* * *

Michael and Tess reached Harvard Square at half past two. There wasn't much time to figure out how to make the meeting with Kit as secure as possible. They didn't even have a chance to begin. As they walked down a side street off Mass Ave, they noticed a crowd that had gathered near a restaurant. There was a police car parked nearby.

Keeping a good distance from the police, Michael and Tess entered the crowd. Accounts of what had happened were being passed along. Someone had been shot. What was the world coming to, the FBI agents and now this?

He was Chinese. Japanese someone corrected. Some said armed. Belonged to the mafia. The Japanese mafia. Maybe it was about drugs. There had been a shooting in a Thai restaurant a while back. The descriptions of the victim varied. Kit didn't seem to fit them.

Moments later several other police cars with their sirens blaring made their way through traffic to the restaurant. Michael and Tess walked away from the crowd back to the appointed meeting place in the Square. Kit didn't show up. Tess called the contact number. There was no message. "What do you know about his girlfriend?" Michael said in response to the news.

"Kit said she had a condo with a great view of the river. We could start there."

"They probably put up a new one every Tuesday around here. Anything else?"

"She drives a bright red Austin Healy."

"That's it?"

Tess nodded.

"Well at least there aren't many of those."

They spent the next three hours scouring the streets and parking garages. They both sensed they'd found it when they spotted a red Austin Healy near two high-rises. Tess smiled. "Is it me, or does that car scream steal me?"

"It's you."

"Come on, that's some spot to leave a car like that. The driver's door isn't even shut."

"I know, I'm just kidding you. Something's off."

"Either that or she gets vintage cars delivered weekly like a magazine subscription."

They got out of the car and walked toward the Austin Healy. "Let's search it," Tess suggested. "She might have left something interesting in it, maybe with her address."

Tess didn't get a response. Michael was thinking about searching another car. Now he remembered there had been traffic noise in the background of Sara's last message. If she had called from her car, maybe she had whatever it was with her.

In a moment, the possibility grew to a certainty in his mind. He wanted more than anything to find her car and search it. It was so stupid he hadn't thought of it. Maybe not just dumb.

Michael realized he didn't want to see where she died. Feel the force of her agony in the twisted metal.

A car drove up interrupting his thoughts. A woman got out. She was in her early thirties, had a resort tan and an excess of style that made a workshirt and jeans seem elegant. She looked suspiciously at Michael and Tess.

"Not a great spot for Sumiko to put her car," Tess said.

"Blame it on that guy who was staying with her. He was using it when he got himself arrested."

Michael and Tess exchanged a worried glance.

"A neighbor saw it. She said the police pulled him over just as he was leaving the building. I wonder what happened. I thought he was okay for a guy." She gave Tess a wink.

"Does Sumiko know about it yet?" Michael asked.

"She's in Japan."

Michael and Tess called the police. There was no record of any such arrest. Everett had gotten Kit. Michael told Tess about his idea of searching Sara's car. He was determined to convey his certainty that it made sense. The sense also included the fact that it was all they had.

* * *

Disregarding the advice of Hollings and the rest of his aides, Shaw flew back to Washington. He was in the air when Pierce delivered his address.

The speech was forceful, calling for tough legislation while cleverly denouncing the militia and Shaw's connection to them without mentioning either by name. He had seized the high ground Pierces aides agreed, pointing to his first positives since Shaw's speech.

Shaw fended off reporters and the curious as he and Laura got off the plane. "It's a national tragedy. I'm sure these criminals will be found and prosecuted to the fullest extent of the law." Then he got the question he knew was coming from a young blogger with nothing to lose.

"Some claim your rhetoric might be encouraging the people behind this attack."

"You want a quote, let me give you one."

The blogger wondered if he was going to be lucky.

"How miserable is the man that governs a people where six parts in seven are poor, indebted, discontented and armed."

"That's pretty strong stuff," the blogger replied smelling a story. "You willing to be quoted?"

"The quote was by a governor of Virginia. Have any idea when he said it?" The reporters drew a blank.

"1676. Three hundred years this has been going on. I think that calls for strong stuff. Instead the President is scapegoating these people, rather than solving their problems."

* * *

Everett's man had his instructions. Twelve hours after the President's speech he was to call in the anonymous tip about the downed plane. Everett gave himself the twelve hours on the chance he would get lucky in the meantime. He was hoping some group with no conceivable connection to him would discover it in the morning.

A bird watching society would have been perfect. Instead a self contained local militia group nobody ever heard of was on night reconnaissance practice, when it came across it around eleven o'clock and notified the local police.

* * *

Michael and Tess were halfway to Philadelphia when they heard the end of a newsflash. "Six bodies were discovered in the plane and over 400,000 dollars on board. The FBI has identified the men as Colombian nationals. At first thought to be drug related, authorities are now looking into a possible connection with the events in Virginia."

"Possible connection," Michael said sarcastically. "Everett probably left everything including their driver's licenses and hat sizes in the green van. It'll turn out they were the ones who did it and Pierce is left looking like a fool blaming the militia. So now we're dealing with Colombian nationals."

"The Puerto Rican salsa band?"

"Everett's favorite. Let me guess. A plane takes off from an airport, one that we're familiar with, crashes in some remote area. An anonymous tip phoned in conveniently after Pierce's speech notifies the police, and suddenly Pierce's election chances crash right along with the plane."

Michael found the start of the news item on another channel. Everything fit except the part about a militia group finding the plane. Michael checked another news source to see if it was reported in error. It wasn't.

"Why would he use the militia?" Tess asked.

Michael didn't have an answer. He was busy cursing the hours it would take to get to Sara's car.

* * *

"Gentlemen I think it's possible we've just seized the low ground," the President began in a heated early morning meeting with Hart and Hilliard. "We've got dead Colombians with a bunch of money, false passports and obvious drug cartel connections."

"Who were found by some militia group, which makes one wonder," Hilliard interrupted.

"The FBI checked them out," Pierce responded. "It doesn't look like they're connected to anybody. I wish they were, because it turns out the Colombians have traces of bomb making material on their clothing. If we've got the wrong folks, we're going to have an uproar over this."

Hart tried to reassure the President. "We have next to no exposure. We didn't say the militia did it or didn't, that was the beauty of the speech."

"And a beauty it was," Pierce added. "But Shaw will pin it on us anyway."

Hilliard tried on a point of view he wasn't exactly thrilled with. "What he'll do is pin himself in a corner with the militia. They haven't got a lot of friends."

"Just noisy ones," Hart added.

Pierce wasn't cheered. "It still isn't our best hour. We have to look into the possibility that Everett and his associates were just running around in the woods and somebody else did this."

"There's too much evidence pointing to the militia," Hart said more out of hope than conviction. It conveyed neither, but he wanted Hilliard to be the one to argue for the worst case scenario. Hilliard reluctantly obliged.

"Maybe it was supposed to look that way. With Everett's background."

"It can't be discounted," Hart added, pleased with his position.

"This isn't Guatemala," Pierce said angrily. "I'll be damned if we'll be destabilized by some ex CIA mercenary. If Everett's involved in Shaw's campaign, that's another reason to be tracking the money."

Pierce turned to Hilliard. "All right Hilliard give me one good I told you so, so I can feel free to light a fire under your ass and the investigation." Hilliard knew better than to seem pleased. Pierce went on. "You have someone in Shaw's camp, why the hell aren't we getting more on the money?"

"We're pushing him hard."

"Your agent's still missing, you haven't found-"

"Flaherty," Hilliard said, filling in the blank for Pierce.

"What's happening with that camera?"

"It was badly burnt before it went into the river, but they're working on it as well as the CDs. The therapist on them could be Flaherty's. There could be a problem of privilege."

"That's swell. But I'm a little more concerned about the privilege of Mister Flaherty's company."

"We're devoting everything we can, but if we short other parts of the investigation we could end up with nothing."

"Meanwhile we've got these Colombians."

"We're due for an update on that from DEA and State," Hart interjected.

"I don't think they're going away," Pierce continued. "What are Flaherty's politics these days? He may be there just to point us in the wrong direction."

Hilliard shook his head. "We've been going over his radio broadcasts. They were exposés on the militia. His partner on the radio show, Sara Ellison, was killed in an auto accident."

"Recently?"

"Right after a broadcast which included a direct reference to Everett."

"Everett?"

"There's more to it. There was actually a death threat on the program, which doesn't seem like Everett's style. We've gotten some files from Ellison's house and we weren't the first to search it. Michael's prints were there along with a woman named Tess Prudhomme. We've got the New Orleans Office working on her background.

"Another thing, the therapist was high ranking German Intelligence and we're already getting contradictory signals about a possible connection with Israel. There might be international implications, I mean besides the Colombians."

Pierce saw the waters getting deeper and murkier. If Everett were orchestrating Shaw's campaign, that's precisely where he wanted Pierce, knee deep and thrashing about.

"What about going public with Flaherty?" the President asked, trying to make it seem like a question, not a demand.

Hilliard knew it wasn't a question. He tried to fend off the demand.

"If there are leaks we might have to. But I still think that's an excellent way of getting him killed. The Bureau's divided on it. If it makes it any easier, the more I think about it, the more I'm sure if he had the Rosetta stone in his pocket, he'd be in here bargaining with it. He's still out there hunting or he's already dead."

CHAPTER 27

Shamans, Saints, and Sinners

It was a little before midnight when Arens parked near Nime's theater. He surveyed the building. "A perfect place to murder him," he thought to himself. He laughed as he considered it. Murder in the Cathedral. After all wasn't this theater a shabby contemporary version of a Cathedral and wasn't the victim a shabby contemporary version of a high priest.

Upstairs Nime was sitting on the edge of the stage, finishing a session by answering questions from a small group of people. An athletic young woman wearing a Harvard sweat shirt under an oversized coat spoke next. "What happens if you speak to someone in a fantasy and they are just negative, all they say are horrible things?"

Nime thought it over. "I think it's clear when we try to address the people in fantasy whether they respond in a human way that brings connection and insight and those that are negative and abusive. We all have negative voices inside. Ignore their message, just ask who is speaking. If they reveal who they are, who put that voice in you, parent, teacher, relative, whoever, it could be very healing. It's like a police proceeding where they've at least identified the culprit. Very helpful."

Arens heard Nime's session going on as he passed by the "Uncle Vanya" literature, found Nime's office on the second floor and began searching it. He set his gun down on Nime's desk and looked over his papers. They included a partially completed manuscript entitled, "Shamans, Saints and Sinners, the Quest for Ecstatic Revelation" and copious handwritten notes.

After the session Nime escorted the group out of theater. They chatted on the street before Nime returned to his office. It was deserted and in disarray. He turned and saw Arens enter, gun in hand, from an adjoining room. Arens started to apologize for the mess.

"As you can see there's nothing to interest you here," Nime angrily interrupted.

"There's your book," Arens responded. "I do hope you include John Dee. You know of him of course?" Nime didn't answer and Arens continued.

"Really a remarkable character. A Renaissance mystic who wanted to learn the language of the angels hoping to save Christianity and a Machiavellian realist who invented the idea of the British Empire and talked Elizabeth the First into creating it."

Arens paused. Not getting a reply he went on. "Of course I was hoping to find a sample of your Intelligence work. Maybe the contact number of your agent, that enterprising redhead. Or something you're sending the Israelis since you've been trying to make up for German guilt all by yourself. For the life of me I don't understand it. Their politics."

"It's true they've grown old and corrupt. One day they'll be young again. I consider my duty to help them survive until then."

"Or maybe it's not just that. There's your family's guilt."

"How would you know? They point you in a direction and you kill."

"I know more about you than you think. Shall I display my ignorance?"

"If that was a question, I would say no."

"Your father left Germany in the thirties because it was unhealthy to be a leading Communist in Hitler's new order. He emigrated to Brazil, bought a plantation, grew bromeliads in Santa Catarina and waited out the war. He met a dancer. She was only part German. Can't blame him for preferring the samba to the polka. He was born nobility, shows what can happen when you don't stick with your class. How am I doing so far?"

"Splendid, if your goal is rehashing common knowledge."

"They were married and you were born. They had problems. Maybe she wanted to be free. Or maybe she found out he wasn't going to be the next Juan Peron. Who knows? She played around and he went native, spending his time collecting bromeliads and tribal cosmologies."

Arens saw Nime eyeing the gun on the desk. Arens moved closer to it and continued.

"It was no situation for a child. He sent you back to

Germany to live with relatives. Your father never came back. Maybe he was still a Communist at heart. Your mother went on with her so called career and her escapades including one with Martin Bormann."

Before Nime could protest Arens went on.

"Of course it's just a nasty rumor. In any case we shouldn't be too hard on her, she had an extraordinarily developed nose for power. After all if the Communists had taken over instead of Hitler, your father might have been a Cabinet Minister. She wasn't very particular about political leanings. There are those who say the same about Herr Bormann. She had a second child, your half sister. Your half sister evidently had her mother's taste in romance because she in turn had a daughter out of wedlock."

Nime tried not to look surprised.

"Surely you've heard all this. The daughter was raised by nuns, and later put up for adoption. No one knows what has happened to her. She ran away, just like her mother."

"It's ancient history."

"You're a psychologist. We're filled head to toe with ancient history. We're lucky if we can manage an occasional foray into the present or the future."

"So who are they pointing you toward now? Me?"

Arens answered by picking up the gun. "Unfortunately I'm not here for 'Uncle Vanya'. You see we're not sure whether Tess is a Mossad agent or just a hireling of yours. But in any case you might be in the position to help us find her. Then there is a woman named Sara Ellison. Unfortunately she's beyond finding, but she might have left something with you."

Nime was silent. There was no use telling Arens honestly that he didn't know where Tess and Michael were. Arens would assume he could figure it out.

At first Nime was not sure Tess was still alive. Then he heard through government contacts that their fingerprints were found at Sara's.

It was very probable that the day Sara was killed she called Michael about the same time she called him. Knowing Sara's habits, he could make a good guess where she'd put her important information. He could see Michael and Tess taking the next step. He could take it himself, but Tess was perfect for the job.

Having his own contacts in the government, Everett would be following the same line of reasoning right to Nime. Arens patiently waited. "We might as well sit down, it looks like it's going to be a long night. On the other hand there's your long lost niece. Perhaps you would be more cooperative if I told you I know who she is." Arens paused for his revelation to sink in. "My deep dark secret for yours."

The night didn't turn out to be long. Aren's got a text from Everett. All that was said was a short banal message, something like "nice weather we are having". It meant Nime was not needed, they had the information they wanted.

Arens was in a good mood when he left the theater building. He didn't like having to kill a philosopher. Like crossword puzzles, philosophers amused him. Unlike crossword puzzles, philosophers were in short supply. He hummed "Some enchanted evening" to himself as he thought ahead. Knowledge is power he knew and he knew where Michael and Tess would be.

* * *

Michael and Tess began the search for Sara's car at the salvage yards. It was the most logical place for a demolished car to end up. Even though it was daylight, they were counting on nobody paying much attention to you unless you bothered them with a question, or had an armful of parts to buy.

Hiking through the aisles of wrecks was time consuming. Their efforts were yielding nothing, and the longer they were at it, the more they worried about being spotted.

Even before they reached the last rows of cars, Tess had a feeling it wasn't going to be there. "You don't suppose they repaired the thing."

"It was too badly damaged," Michael quickly responded. No sooner than he said it, he rethought it. "It was Jack's gift to Sara and she loved it. Maybe he decided to save it."

There were two body shops that specialized in repairing Volvos. The personnel would have been more watchful than the ones at the salvage yards, but fortunately the shops were closed on Saturday. It was just a matter of breaking in and locating the car.

Michael was shocked when he saw it. The body had been completely restored. He wasn't ready to see it twisted and bent. But even less ready to see this.

He got in the car and sat in the driver's seat. He expected to sense something of her, her terror, a whiff of perfume, a dying echo of a heartbeat. There was just metal, leather and the smell of fresh paint. There didn't seem to be a trace. But then life isn't so interested in traces. It uses what it can and moves on.

That's what makes finding them an art. The trace might be a faint radio signal from the start of everything 10 billion years ago. It might be recorded in the rocks or an old newspaper, or in the funny way a person smiles. There's always a trace.

They began to go over the car. Michael went through the trunk while Tess checked the glove compartment. Michael got into the driver's seat and began to search under the seat, as Tess took the ash tray out. It was filled with potpourri. Michael noticed Tess take a small portion of it and smell it. "Sara treated herself to the smell after she quit smoking."

As Tess put the ash tray back, something shifted in it. She reached into the bottom of the potpourri and touched some-thing metallic. Michael was searching under the seat when he heard Tess say, "I think she also treated herself to a safety deposit key."

Tess excitedly handed the safety deposit key to Michael. "She obviously used it regularly. Of course she could have just gotten a kick out of visiting her diamonds."

Michael smiled, but he was already formulating a plan. "She probably built up a whole file of papers. We can get Jack to open the safety deposit box."

Jack had said at the funeral that he and the kids were going to stay at his parent's house. Michael called their number. He got an answering machine and was about to leave a message when Jack picked up. A children's cable show was going in the background. It didn't cover up the edge in Jack's voice.

"Michael," Jack said as if the word had a bitter taste. It seemed to clear his palate. "I'm sorry for the tone. Actually I'm glad you called. Sara should have never been involved, but nevertheless you'll have to excuse some of my behavior. You were right about the accident. That bomb in our backyard made it pretty obvious."

"Forget it, I'm sorry about it all."

"I appreciate that. What can I do?"

Michael had the safety deposit key in his hand. "I can't go into it all on the phone. But the FBI shootings and what happened to Sara are connected. She had some important information. I think she kept it in her safety deposit box and I need you to get it."

Michael arranged to meet Jack at the Englander motel. It wasn't nearby, but he knew the Indian owner and his wife and that meant two less people he might have to worry about should things get sticky.

Jack hung up the phone. The wall facing him was covered with framed photographs. One of them was a picture of a platoon in Vietnam. Everett and Richard Coulter were in it.

CHAPTER 28

A nightmare

Tess checked into the motel while Michael waited in the car, figuring the less public exposure the better. He was sure by now the government will have plastered his face all over the media. He nervously looked around. He had been preoccupied with the key on the drive. He wondered if he had been as diligent as he should have been in making sure they weren't being followed. He was relieved to see nobody was in sight.

* * *

If the President had wanted clarity, he wasn't getting it. He was told that the FBI had searched Randy Hastings house. They found a fishing trip letter, history books and Civil War memorabilia from a store called Articles of Confederation. They also determined that Everett and the six men associated with him were participating in a small town bowling tournament at the time of the attack.

The information coming in on the Colombians was suggestive, but not conclusive. The FBI traced the men to a motel where they stayed, apparently posing as a musical group. The search of the room and the phone records yielded nothing. Nobody at the truck rental in Georgia which rented the vans could remember them, and the rental paper work was also a dead end.

Then the NSA came up with a bombshell, the cellphone conversations of several Colombian drug cartel figures. One of the conversations included their expletive laced feelings about the US government's interference in their business and references to an upcoming attack on Washington. It also included a reference to the nickname of one of the men found in the plane.

The President knew he would have to respond quickly. Despite his clever speech, he would still be blamed for targeting the wrong people. Not that he didn't believe that Everett and the militia were also involved, but the proof would be slow in coming.

It called for a bold stroke, not considered Pierce's strong suit. It was all the more surprising to his aides when he asked for a draft of a Black Forest speech. It would outline the government's long commitment to the research and express his decision to go forward with its implementation.

The President's aides were dumfounded. Until recently all their efforts were aimed at shooting down the idea. But not being able to shoot it down was one thing, taking it on yourself quite another. They knew Pierce of all people would not be pursuing this without rock solid scientific backing. He assured them he had it.

With the proviso that the NSA revelation would stand up, they came around to praising the move as brilliant. It would outflank Shaw on the issue, help quiet the uproar, and show character and decisiveness in a critical hour.

The best part of it was that Pierce wouldn't be stuck with having to pursue it after he won the election. He could satisfy the public by using it as leverage to gain huge concessions from drug enforcement in Colombia, Peru, Mexico and all over the world. Having explained this last bit of practical politics to a man renowned for being practical, the aides awaited his congratulatory response.

Pierce nodded in agreement, but he had other ideas. He didn't know why he was being handed a page in the history books, but he knew he would take it.

* * *

A photograph of Michael filled the television screen in the Englander motel office. Satya, the owner's wife didn't notice. Her attention was elsewhere. She had turned the sound off when the last customer came in, and hadn't turned it back on. She was nervously fidgeting with paperwork at the front desk. She dropped the inlaid letter opener she was using as her husband entered from the adjacent living quarters. The TV caught his eye.

At the same moment Michael and Tess were in their motel room absorbing the shock of seeing the newsflash. "ABC news has learned from reliable sources that Michael Flaherty, an ex DEA agent linked to the killing of a Georgia Patrolman, is now being sought by Federal authorities in connection with the recent shootings in Virginia."

"We have George Hilliard to thank for that. There goes my-" Michael started to joke when the phone rang.

"Don't answer it," Michael warned. The telephone stopped ringing.

"Let's get the hell out of here," Tess urged. There was a knock at the door. "There's no way it's Jack," Tess said shaking her head.

Tess waited until Michael grabbed his gun. She pulled her gun out of her purse and went to the door. Another knock. Tess tensed.

"Ms Richards, Ms Richards, this is Satya."

Tess was relieved to hear her voice and opened the door a crack. Satya was alone, looking embarrassed. Michael heard Satya say, "I'm sorry to have to ask you to come to the office, but part of the registration was incomplete." The door closed as Tess went out.

The two women returned to the motel office. Satya apologized for the inconvenience and handed Tess a registration form. As Tess started to fill it out, she noticed that the TV was turned off. Satya cast an anxious glance toward the open door to the living quarters behind her to the left. Her eyes began to tear.

"Something wrong?" Tess asked.

Satya was almost paralyzed, fighting an enormous inner struggle. "Go," she said weakly.

Tess was bewildered. "I don't understand."

Satya gathered her nerve. "Just go," she managed to say as she looked toward the open door with obvious dread. Tess glanced at the doorway. "Before he," Satya continued, but no further word sounded.

Tess went for the gun in her purse. Her hand nervously tightened on the trigger as she pointed it toward the doorway. A young man appeared in it.

Norman Rockwell could have painted him. He had All American boyish good looks, freckled complexion and jet black hair. Tess had no conscious memory of seeing his gun as she fired. The thought it was all a horrible mistake entered her mind, and a split second later was driven from it by the sound of his gun firing.

Tess' bullet hit him in the shoulder as his shot wounded Satya. He staggered backwards. Tess rushed toward him, screaming and firing wildly, trying to finish him off.

He scrambled into the living room where Satya's husband and young son were bound and gagged. Tess entered firing at point blank range, but her gun was empty. He lunged forward, grabbing her arm, pulling her down.

The two grappled, ripping and tearing at each other. She grabbed a brass lamp and beat him in the head with it. Over and over. He grabbed the cord. He yanked it tightly around Tess' neck and began to choke her. He forced her on her back and sat above her, strangling the life out of her.

Tess saw his face twisted in a sadistic grin as the cord tightened around her neck. It got very quiet as she began to lose consciousness. Her thoughts strangely continued, but were no longer connected to action. "I'm going to die and his horrible face is the last thing I'm ever going to see."

"No air, losing it," she realized as his features became distorted, almost hallucinatory. She saw his grinning mouth sprout a darting tongue, adding a horrific lewd touch to his malevolent face. But the tongue was metallic and sharp edged. And there was a tiny rivulet of blood dripping from it. A blade protruded from his mouth as his eyes widened and glazed over. Tess screamed and jerked her head out of the way.

He toppled forward. There was a letter opener driven through the back of his head. Michael was standing above him. He pulled the dead body off of Tess. Shaking in horror, she hugged Michael. He comforted her and then started to untie the others.

Tess' shock turned to rage. She grabbed Michael's gun and fired shots into her assailant's lifeless body. Michael restrained her, taking back the gun.

"We've got to get out of here, the police!"

The two drove away from the motel. Tess suddenly asked Michael to pull over. She got out of the car and walked to the side of the road. Michael saw her doubled over, throwing up. He got out of the car, but she motioned to him that she was all right.

The two continued on. Michael noticed with concern that Tess was still upset. "You want to talk?"

"I really thought he was going to kill me. I've been close to dying before, but this was different."

"Maybe you're different?" Michael offered.

Tess pulled herself together. "Who the hell was that guy?"

"Probably militia," Michael answered. "Somebody working for Everett."

"And how the hell did he find us? Jack set us up?"

It was a thought Michael couldn't contend with and quickly dismissed. "That's crazy, these people killed Sara."

Tess didn't dismiss the idea as readily but offered another. "His phone could have been tapped."

"It's possible, but it's more likely we were followed."

Tess shook her head in disbelief. "Great alternatives, this is a nightmare."

The reality of it sank in. "We haven't much time, but we've got this," Michael finally said as he held up the safety deposit key. "You got any ideas on how we could use it?"

"Sure I've got an idea, it's my business to have ideas like that. If I rented a box, that would get me inside."

"You still need the bank key. The teller opens the other lock."

"Maybe I can save her the trouble."

CHAPTER 29

An ever expanding sense of self and a Cuban
cigar

Hollings didn't take Shaw's coolness over the phone too seriously. Friction between Shaw and himself was nothing new. You couldn't go through what they had without real bouts of it. All you could hope is to keep to the issues, and not let the skeletons in the closet come out and do a dance macabre.

Shaw was just finishing a pep talk to supporters who were setting up his campaign headquarters in Austin when Hollings walked in. Shaw cut short his remarks, and the workers got the message that the two men wanted to be alone.

"I hear you've been talking to some friends," Shaw began, trying to retain a casual warmth in his voice.

"I have lots of friends," Hollings replied as nonchalantly as he could manage.

"You do, but you know who I'm talking about."

"They wanted to talk to me. They're worried about you."

"What about Pierce? This Colombian thing has opened the door for Black Forest. He might just go through it."

"They think he's afraid of his own shadow. It's you they're concerned with."

"Me?"

"They think you're crazy enough to do it. I keep reassuring them you're not going to win this time."

"That is reassuring," Shaw said sarcastically. "What about next time?"

"I've convinced them you'll be older and wiser."

"Older I can't seem to help, but wiser like that I hope I never am. I don't mean to be overly inquisitive but how much do you tell them?"

"As little as I can and still keep them happy and you alive."

Shaw shook his head disapprovingly. "You've always had a finger in every pot."

Hollings had a ready answer. "Right, and you get to find out what everybody's cooking. Or would you prefer operating in the dark?"

"A friend to all, enemy to none, it's a neat balancing act. I don't know why I trust you."

"We go back to when it counted. Besides you don't trust me. You tell me next to nothing about the whole Everett side of the campaign, and believe me it shows. We've got a royal mess on our hands."

"I don't know that much more than you. That's the way he works."

"You trust him?"

"I do. I know his politics."

"Talk about a finger in every pot. You've got to wonder."

"We're talking about the Presidency of the United States," Shaw said with finality.

* * *

Michael and Tess were driving a newly "acquired" Land Rover as they approached Sara's bank. Tess was dressed to look "pregnant" and disguised with a wig, while Michael had on a baseball cap and sunglasses. He finished going over a profile of Everett's men, with the admonition that Tess should leave immediately if any of them were there or there was any sign of the police.

She told him not to worry. This job like all the others had the calculated precision of a chess game. Every possible move and counter-move was considered. She proceeded only if she had a response for every crucial outcome.

What if Everett's men were there? The police? What was her legal vulnerability at each step of the way? What if the teller returns? What if she were discovered?

She knew under no circumstances would she be found with the bank keys. She also knew how Sara's papers might be passed as her own. When she was younger she thought it out awkwardly and painstakingly from beginning to end, but now it came to her instinctively.

"That's bullshit," Michael responded.

"Not as much as you think."

"I think you've never done a job like this before. You're defiant and reckless and a natural and have reasons all your own for going in there. Just be careful."

The bank was located in the middle of the block. Michael parked across from it. He surveyed the street. Noonday crowds. No sign of the police or Everett's people. An ambulance was parked fifty feet ahead of them.

Michael got out of the car to check it out. Pretending to window shop he looked it over. The driver was the picture of relaxed contentment as he read a dog-eared paperback while he ate his way through a rib lunch.

"I'm glad someone in the world is relaxed," Michael said to Tess when he came back and described the driver. He made a mental note to keep an eye on the ambulance. It'd be a shame to ruin the driver's lunch, but it could come in handy if they had to make an escape. He handed Tess the safety deposit key.

"Good luck."

"Luck better not have anything to do with it."

Inside the bank Tess satisfied herself that the few customers and the personnel were not a problem. She purchased a safety deposit box from a woman teller.

Tess sized her up as they went through the transaction. Late thirties, divorced, been at the bank long enough to get a little sloppy about routines, carries bank keys in right pocket, easily flattered and distracted. Tess noted her physical habits, boundaries, blind spots. All this was done effortlessly thanks to her experience.

As the teller escorted Tess to the safety deposit area, Tess concluded her evaluation. Nothing much happens in this woman's life and she isn't expecting it to.

"So, when are you due?" the teller asked.

"Three months."

"Your first?"

"Yes, I'm really kind of nervous about it," Tess replied, thinking that might cover her if she got any real nerves.

She stopped suddenly. The security officer for the bank emerged from a back office with the bank manager. Tess got closer to the teller to shield herself from their view. She had promised to get the hell out, but she didn't. To Tess' right was the room that housed the safety deposit boxes. They entered it.

Michael was impatiently checking his watch when he saw a police car pull up in front of the bank. Michael looked ahead at the ambulance. He began formulating a plan.

Inside the safety deposit room, Tess opened one lock, and watched as the teller opened the other. The teller handed Tess her key and the strongbox, and put the set of bank keys in her right pocket.

"Just let me know when you're done."

"Thank you. I will just be..."

Tess' voice trailed off as she appeared faint. She started to fall. "Oh, my God," the teller exclaimed and then called to the other room. "Someone, help!" The flustered teller practically grabbed Tess in a bear hug to steady her.

Tess adroitly stole the woman's keys.

"I'll be fine," Tess said, recovering somewhat as the teller grabbed a chair and assisted her. The bank manager entered with the security officer, who stared at Tess.

"I'm fine really," she assured them.

"Would you like some water?" the teller asked.

"You're sweet, but no thanks. I really feel better."

Again reassuring the teller she was all right, Tess got up and walked into the adjoining room with the strongbox. She entered a viewing cubicle. She knew she had to make her move before the teller's next customer.

She pulled out the bank keys from her pocket and opened the cubicle door slightly. She watched as the teller walked away, but the manager and the security officer hadn't budged.

Tess closed the cubicle door. She looked as if she was trying to will them to leave. The teller was about to go on a break when a customer walked up holding a safety deposit key.

On the street a police car pulled to a stop behind Michael. He glanced in the rear view mirror at it. Something odd about the occupants? Were they police or Everett's men planning another deadly phony arrest?

Michael knew he couldn't wait to find out. He quickly got out of his car and walked up to the ambulance with his plan playing in his head. A fire was required. He knew which way the fire trucks would come. They'd block the street and both police cars. Michael pulled his gun, opened the passenger's door and got in.

"I don't carry any drugs," the ambulance driver said casually as if this sort of thing happened every day.

"I need the ambulance."

"And I need an ever expanding sense of self and a Cuban cigar. But at least you get your ambulance."

Michael got on his cell. He called the fire department. He was surprised to hear someone else had already reported the fire. How do two people call in a fire that doesn't even exist? went through his mind. "Who else called it in?" he reflexively asked. "He had an accent," was the only reply.

Inside the bank cubicle Tess picked up the strongbox and opened the door a crack. The manager and the cop were standing with their backs to her. She weighed the chances of them leaving against the chances of the teller coming back. She walked quickly into the safety deposit room.

As the teller and the customer headed for the safety deposit area, Tess went to Sara's compartment. She set down her own box, quickly inserted the bank key and Sara's key and opened the compartment. The manager and the officer were still talking as the teller let the customer through the security gate.

Tess pulled out the box and lifted the lid. She had a moment of elation at seeing file folders when she heard the teller from the next room. Tess stuffed the file folders under her ample clothing, hurriedly replaced the box and swung the compartment door nearly closed.

Locking it shut would just take seconds. There were none as the teller and the customer were coming toward her. The teller began reaching into her right pocket for the bank key.

Tess stepped toward her, concealing the partially opened compartment behind her.

The teller was puzzled the keys weren't in her pocket. The officer and the manager walked over to the teller as she started to check her other pocket.

"Hold it there," the officer said unfastening his gun. "I want to see you." Everybody stopped.

The officer motioned to the customer. Tess glanced over at him. She could see that he resembled Michael. As the officer began interrogating him, the teller was momentarily distracted. Tess seized the opportunity.

"Can I talk to you?" she asked the teller.

"Certainly."

"It's personal," Tess said, moving closer to the teller as if she wanted to whisper what she had to say. Tess put her hand lightly on the woman's right arm and captured her full attention with a desperately earnest look.

"It's about my husband. This morning I found out he's having an affair."

"Oh my God."

"With my sister."

Agony suddenly replaced the teller's professional smile as tears came to her eyes. Tess had expected a distracting moment of sympathy in which to make her move.

Instead she had hit a nerve and was distracted herself by the woman's sudden intensity. Fortunately the woman made it simple. She hugged Tess, who quickly dropped the keys in the teller's left pocket.

"I know how much you've been hurt," the woman said.

A strange feeling that the woman really knew filled Tess. It was both comforting and disturbing. Tess withdrew from the hug.

"Thanks, I feel better just telling someone," Tess heard herself say in character. The emptiness of the words somehow bothered her.

The teller "found" the keys in her left pocket, put back Tess' box and she and Tess turned to leave. Behind them Sara's open compartment was visible as they passed the security officer still questioning the customer.

Tess started to walk toward the exit. She was hurrying as inconspicuously as she could. She heard the officer's voice behind her call out for her to stop. She kept going, pretending not to hear him. He yelled to her again and drew his gun.

The exit seemed to recede from Tess as adrenaline rushed and time dilated in her anxiety. Split seconds in which to decide should she gamble he wouldn't shoot her in the back before she walked through it. The fire department rushed in right by her shouting to everyone to clear the bank. Tess escaped in the confusion.

Tess hurried from the bank through a chaos of panicked customers, firefighters and men in police uniform. She glanced around quickly, but there was no sign of Michael. She knew the security officer would be out any moment. Suddenly the ambulance's siren wailed. Her attention was riveted on it.

"Get in!" the ambulance driver yelled to her.

Tess had no time to think it over. She got in as the vehicle sped off. She looked at the driver with a mixture of puzzlement and paranoia until Michael appeared from the back. The ambulance sped off. Michael looked behind them. The police cars were blocked by the sea of fire engines and nobody was following.

Michael and Tess left the ambulance driver with a long walk, a short explanation and a kiss on the cheek from Tess for his trouble. He really didn't need an explanation, Nime had supplied that.

Tess acquired a new car after they abandoned the ambulance. She drove as Michael started examining the files. She smiled at him. "That was a nice move, calling out the fire department."

"Thanks. But I wasn't the only one." The two shared a moment of puzzlement before Michael resumed reading. He was pleased with what he was finding. "This is very detailed. Sara definitely had a high level source."

"Can you tell who?" Tess asked as she reminded herself to keep their speed down.

Michael rapidly flipped through the pages.

"Judging from the different sorts of information there might be more than one. There's stuff in here from Nime. He thanks Sara for her info and will pass it on."

"And?" Tess said impatiently.

"Doesn't say. But it's obvious he's still in the trade."

Michael scanned more pages."It gets better and better. Whoever supplied this must have been inner circle." What Michael read next stopped him cold.

"I can't believe this, Richard Coulter was involved."

"Who's Richard Coulter?"

"Sara's father in law."

"Her own family?" Tess said turning toward Michael in shock. She saw Michael nod.

"That's what she was calling to tell me about. Money went from his group to Everett to the militia and Shaw."

"And she knew this and her family killed her?!"

For a moment Michael let in the horror of that possibility. "Unless Everett was on his own. Or even one of his men. That's operating procedure. No one's accountable."

"So we'll make him accountable. That will be our operating procedure."

"There are plenty off leads here. But Everett's not going to wait around for us to put this together. I'm sure he's already heading out of the country. Which is what we should be doing. I want to do the negotiations with Hilliard and the government from a safe distance."

"You're going to leave his fate to them?"

"They'll never get the chance. We'll make him such a liability his friends will kill him."

CHAPTER 30

Freedom or revenge

Michael made arrangements for the safekeeping of copies of the documents. He and Tess crossed the border into Canada. They picked up fake passports and visas from a specialist Tess knew in Montreal. His dream remained forging art works, but this was still his bread and butter.

The Montreal international airport was crowded with afternoon commuters. Michael and Tess had picked the time in the hopes that the crush of passengers would provide cover and distraction. They merged with the crowd as they made their way to an escalator.

A rifle scope found them from a high angle and began tracking them. They momentarily disappeared into the crowd. Another scope immediately picked them up. They reached the escalator and ascended.

At the top of the escalator the family in front of them lifted their two small children off of it and turned to their left. That opened a clear line of sight for Michael and Tess that included Russell Everett.

He appeared out of a group of people and stepped toward them. A shock wave of recognition and hatred hit them both as they went for their guns.

"There's three rifles on you," Everett warned.

Tess pointed her gun at Everett. "I couldn't care less. I'm ready to go, are you?"

"Quite, but you'll only get other people killed."

"That shouldn't concern you," Michael said with venom.

"Let's move," Tess said motioning with her gun.

"Why not?" Everett replied. "If you're interested in slaughter, we can at least keep it private."

The three stepped away from the passing crowd as it rushed by them, oblivious to what was happening. "I'm more interested in talking," Everett continued. "Kit told us about your forger and-"

"You killed him," Tess interrupted, threatening Everett with her gun.

Everett didn't miss a beat. "You want me to finish or do you want to finish this now?"

"Go on," Michael said.

"You undoubtedly have Sara's papers tucked away with a friend or encrypted on the internet, so you can play footsy with Pierce from across the Atlantic. And I thought before you foul things up in your typical fashion you might want to know the truth."

"The truth is what's about to ruin Coulter's breakfast and your health."

"The truth is her sources had connections to the mafia."

"Bullshit," Michael said loudly but a little unsuredly.

"Hollings been cozy with them for years. They wanted to destroy Shaw and Black Forest so they threatened him. Not his life, he wouldn't have buckled, but they threatened to kill Shaw. Enter your light fingered redhead. I'm still not sure whether the mob chose her to steal Hollings' attache case or Sara's friend Nime."

Michael gave Tess a questioning look as Everett went on.

"It's just a theory, I don't want to cause any unnecessary domestic strife. Nime wanted to stop Shaw at all costs and I know he had some mafia assets. It's ironic. You almost gave your life for the DEA and now you're helping drug dealers."

"That's novel, a new found morality."

"Nothing has changed. You still don't begin to know."

"Enough to realize that Hollings or Nime may have been responsible for the theft, but there's no way they could have gotten all the stuff in Sara's files. That had to come from some-body in close. Close to you, close to Coulter."

Everett didn't say anything as Michael thought it over. "It was Jack, wasn't it? He thought it would stop his father before he got in deep."

Everett took a moment to respond. "I don't propose to get between father and son. I am convinced Jack wouldn't have passed that information unless he mistakenly thought we were somehow involved in what happened to Sara."

"Mistaken. You killed her."

"Don't be obscene. Sara was killed by that freckle-faced gentleman you skewered in the motel."

"A militia goon of yours."

"He was an insane criminal who liked the word militia better than racist bank robber. I had nothing to do with killing Sara. I can prove it to you any time you want. Of course then you'd have to give up your ridiculous vendetta."

"You never kill anybody," Tess nearly spat at Everett. "What about Kit?"

"We're the only reason he's still alive. He's got almost as many enemies as you do. After the robbery we assumed that Tess and he worked for...well let's say we made some assumptions. But it turns out Kit and I have a lot more in common than I ever imagined. And I believed what he told us about you. So it turns out you two don't know anything that would cause me any problems."

Tess pointed her gun at him."We've got plenty of problems for you, starting with this."

"Sara's papers will cause us some grief, if that's what you want. But it comes down to this. My friends and I were bowling the night of the attack. When the FBI unearths our green vans they'll find they were part of our survivalist training and were filled with canned food. The government will sweep it all under the rug along with the charges against you. Pierce has his Colombians and his place in history doing Black Forest."

Michael responded sharply. "The last time I looked, this country wasn't built on, we hold these half truths to be self evident."

"Does Pierce want the truth? He's a pragmatist. The truth is what's simple and keeps him President. You'll just muck up the works. I gambled he wouldn't do Black Forest and lost. Shaw will have other issues."

"I'm sure you've already seen to that."

"Why not? He's actually trying to do something. You'd wait until the American dream's a memory and nobody's safe but the rich. Hopefully before then you'll wake up and carry the torch. I'll leave you two to sort out your secrets. I have a country to save." Everett waved off his marksmen and started to leave.

"Everett!" Tess yelled out.

Everett stopped and faced her. Tess raised her gun and pointed it at him. Everett stared at her. "It's your choice, freedom or revenge."

Revenge was close and freedom was not as Tess' hand tightened on the trigger. Michael reached over and grabbed Tess' arm, deflecting her aim from Everett. She started to turn to Michael with a look of betrayal when she saw Kit walk up.

He smiled at her. His smile was full of the pleasure of reunion and friendship and still had room for something more. It seemed to offer up something extraordinary to her. She was trying to read it as he and Everett turned and walked away, disappearing into the crowd.

* * *

Coulter was passed the news of what might happen. The sky wouldn't fall, but they would definitely get rained on.

They had some factors in their favor in their effort to head it off. Sara's files contained disinformation that Everett managed to get in through Hollings after he learned of Hollings' duplicity. Maybe enough manure to make the whole thing stink. And they had their own files on people in Pierce's camp.

Coulter went to his study and began reading one of his favorite books on history. Accounts of others facing its ebbs and flows would prepare him for what was to come.

* * *

Nime thought he'd be asked to go to Paris to contact Tess and Michael. He made it clear with his connection to Sara that he considered himself ideal for the task, but was told other agents led by Eilat Harel would handle it.

Now Nime made up his mind to go to South America. It was time to return, made obvious by his reaction to Arens' offer to tell him who his niece was.

It was small satisfaction that he told Arens nothing about Michael or Sara despite his offer and threats. He wondered if he would have been steadfast the long night if Arens hadn't received Everett's message. "All's well" he reminded himself.

Nime collected his writings that he was going to bring with him and prepared for the trip. The woman he was searching for was scheduling no such trip. After her husband's campaign she had other plans.

* * *

It had rained the night before in Paris. The next morning as Michael made his way from the metro stop at the Place de la

Concorde to the American Embassy he noticed the brilliant blue sky. Too glorious he thought for all the enterprises that go on below it.

He reconsidered. Well after all we're blood made from the stars. Some mix.

His rehearsals of the upcoming meeting were built around dealing with a hard nosed negotiator. He could see himself first giving him an earful about his betrayal by the National Security establishment and then storming out. It didn't happen that way.

Pierce wanted Sara's papers badly. He knew Michael was difficult to deal with and handpicked the negotiator. The meeting was protracted, but the negotiator was conciliatory. Michael got an apology of sorts for his betrayal and was not pressured to have his debriefing go beyond what he wanted to reveal.

Each side got most of what they wanted. Pierce got Sara's papers and Michael's agreement to be silent about the affair. Shaw's campaign was crippled, guaranteeing that Pierce had smooth sailing to the Presidency. Michael had the government's guarantee of immunity, some money and a feeling that a bitter part of his past had finally some resolution.

The night before Tess had kidded him about the small amount of money the government would offer. "I know you want me to change my ways, but I think you're going to have to change yours. You'll pick it up in no time."

Leaving the embassy Michael stopped at a kiosk near the Seine. The newspapers had headlines about Pierce and Black

Forest. There were photographs of Pierce in front of a research facility in Beltsville, Maryland. Michael knew it wasn't where the research would take place, but maintained secrecy and was an imposing building for a photo op.

Michael studied a paper for a moment and then continued walking. Further along the street he bought some roses.

From a distance he saw Tess talking to children by the river's edge. As he approached, the children ran off to their mother. Michael handed Tess the roses.

She was touched, but tenderness was too rare and strong to take straight. She started to say, "If you're asking me to eavesdrop," when he kissed her and they embraced.

They walked along the Seine at the same time together and alone. Tess couldn't help thinking about Kit's smile and what it meant. Michael was wondering how his life would change. Each confined by their own thoughts, each hoping the splendor of the day would prevail.

The End

www.ingramcontent.com/pod-product-compliance
Lightning Source LLC
Chambersburg PA
CBHW050503260626
47157CB00004B/1174